ONE

You can open an envelope and take out something which bites or stings, though it isn't a living creature. I had a letter like that from Franz today. 'Dear Sanna,' he writes, 'I want to see you again, so I may be coming to Frankfurt. I haven't been able to write for some time, but I've been thinking about you a lot. I'm sure you knew that, I'm sure you could feel it. All my love, dear Sanna, from Franz.'

What's happened to Franz? Is he ill? Maybe I should have got straight on a train and gone to him in Cologne. But I didn't. I folded the letter up very small and put it down the neck of my dress, where it still is, scratchy in between my breasts.

I feel tired. Today was so eventful, and such a strain. Life generally is, these days. I don't want to do any more thinking. In fact I *can't* do any more thinking. My brain's all full of spots of light and darkness, circling in confusion.

I'd like to sit and drink my beer in peace, but when I hear the words World Outlook I know there's trouble ahead. Gerti ought not to go provoking an SA man like that, saying the soldiers of the Regular Army, the *Reichswehr*, have nicer uniforms and are better-looking too, and if she absolutely had to pick a military man of some kind she'd rather a Reichswehr soldier than a Stormtrooper. Naturally, such remarks act on Kurt Pielmann like a swarm of angry hornets, stinging him badly – and though the wounds may not be mortal, he'll still turn nasty. I can tell.

Yes, Kurt Pielmann is suddenly looking very sick, and he was so cheerful just now you could almost feel sorry for him. After all, he got another pip three days ago, and he came from Würzburg to Frankfurt today specially to see Gerti, and the Führer. Because the Führer, no less, was in Frankfurt today, to gaze gravely down on the people from the Opera House, and attend a tattoo put on by men who've recently joined up again. I'm going to stand us all another round of beer, by way of a distraction. I hope I've got enough money.

'Waiter!' The place is frantically busy this evening. 'Waiter! Oh, Herr Kulmbach, would *you* call him, please? You can make yourself heard better. And do drink up – yes, four more export beers, please, waiter, and –' But he's off again already.

'Could you by any chance spare another cigarette, Herr Kulmbach?' I don't want Herr Kulmbach to hear Gerti talking to Kurt Pielmann in such a dangerous way, so I keep chattering away at him, anything that comes into my head, just to keep his mind off them. I listen to my own babbling with one ear, while with the other I hear the row brewing up between Gerti and Pielmann.

If I stop talking for just a moment, there's such a roar of voices around me that I feel tired enough to drop.

We're sitting in the Henninger Bar. There's a smell of beer and cigarette smoke, and a lot of loud laughter. You can see the lights of the Opera House Square through the window. They look a little dim and weary, like gaudy yellow flowers which finally feel like folding up and going to sleep.

Gerti and I have been out and about since three this afternoon. I've been friends with Gerti ever since I came to live in Frankfurt. I've been here a year now.

Gerti looks lovely, sitting there with her breasts all blue. Well, not actually her breasts, of course, only the dress over them, but she always looks as if she doesn't have anything on. In Gerti, however, that doesn't seem at all indecent, because she carries herself and talks in such a bright, lively way, she doesn't act at all mysterious. Her thick, fair hair shines, her bright blue eyes shine, her face shines with a rosy glow.

I don't shine at all. I expect that's why Gerti likes me so much. Even though she says I could look very good, I just don't know how to make the best of myself. Gerti and Liska both go on at me about it, and I'm sure they honestly *would* like me to make the best of myself. I would too, but I can never quite manage it.

When I look in the mirror before I go to bed at night, I sometimes do think I look very pretty. I like my skin, because it's so smooth and white. And my eyes seem large and grey and mysterious, and I don't believe there can be a film star in the world with such long, black lashes. At times like this I feel like opening the window and calling out to all the men in the street to come and admire my beauty. I could never really do such a thing, of course. Still, it's a shame if someone's so often at her prettiest when she's alone. Or perhaps I'm only imagining it. At any rate, when I'm with Gerti I feel small and pale and peaky. Even my hair doesn't shine. It's a kind of dull blonde colour.

I shouldn't have ordered those beers – now Herr Kulmbach is following them up with a round of kirsch. Herr Kulmbach is a waiter in the 'Squirrel', and when waiters go out to other bars and restaurants they almost always order lavishly.

'Here's to you, Herr Kulmbach!' 'And the Führer!' Today is a wonderful day, says Kulmbach; today has been a very special experience for the people of Frankfurt.

A couple of SS men at the next table glance across at us and raise their glasses, whether to Gerti or the Führer I'm not sure. Perhaps they're drunk and are raising their glasses to everyone in the world, except, of course, Jews, Social Democrats, Russians, Communists, the French, and suchlike people.

I am busy telling Kulmbach I've been in Frankfurt for a year. I was born in Lappesheim, on the Mosel. 'That's my home, and of course you never forget your home, do you, Herr Kulmbach?' I'm nineteen now; Gerti is a little older. I got to know her through Liska, because Liska works with handicrafts, and Gerti's mother and father have a handicrafts shop in the best part of Frankfurt. Gerti helps in the shop. My father has a public house in Lappesheim, and three vineyards, though they're not in the very best position. In summer, when the vines are in flower and there's a gentle breeze, and the warm sun is shining, the whole world smells of honey. The Mosel is a happy, sparkling snake of a river, with little white boats on it letting the sunbeams pull them downstream. 'And the mountains on the opposite bank, Herr Kulmbach – well, you have to cross on the ferry and get quite close before you realize they *are* mountains. Seen from our pub, they look like great green curly heads, all warm and friendly, so you want to stroke them. But when you get near them you don't find any soft green curls, you find tough trees covered with leaves. And if you climb the mountain you come to the Hunsrück range. It's colder up there than down by the Mosel, and the people are poorer. The children look pale and hungry. The flowers aren't so brightly coloured up in the mountains, and they're much smaller – it's the same with the apples and pears, and there are no vines at all.'

I think of the mountains that look like nice, curly green heads from a distance, and they make me think of my hands. I kept on rubbing Liska's marvellous skin cream in, thinking that would make my skin wonderfully silky, but Algin's got a magnifying glass, and when I put one of my hands under it I got quite a shock. A freckle on my hand looked like a cowpat. Who wants to look at a thing like that? Magnifying glasses ought not to be allowed.

My name is Susanne. Susanne Moder, but I'm called Sanna. I like it when people shorten my name, because it shows they like me. If you're never called anything but your full baptismal name, you are often rather unpopular.

Franz could say it more lovingly than anyone. 'Sanna.' Probably because he thinks in the same slow, soft sort of way. Will he really come? Does he still love me? In a minute I'll go to the Ladies and read his letter again.

I wonder what his mother's up to now? Horrible Aunt Adelheid. Something ought to be done about her; why didn't I do it? As a child, I certainly *would* have paid her out somehow, and it wouldn't have been any laughing matter. That cow. When you grow up you accept things much more meekly, you go soft. We always got our revenge for shabby treatment as children, and quite right too!

Aunt Adelheid is totally uneducated, but she puts on amazing airs. She had several reasons for disliking me. In the first place, she disliked me because my father sent me to secondary school in Koblenz. He was in favour of children getting some learning. I'm not all that keen on learning, myself; didn't have the right sort of head for it. But Algin did, and you only have to look at him to see where learning will get a person.

Algin Moder's my stepbrother, and a famous writer, and seventeen years older than me. His real name is Alois, but he changed it off his own bat, because Alois is more of a name for a humorous writer, which he isn't.

When Algin's mother died, my father married again. His new wife had me. My mother died young too, but my father couldn't help it, he was always good to his wives. Then he married for the third time, a sandy-haired woman from Cochem. Well, being a man *and* the landlord of a pub, my father can't manage without a wife. This one's still alive. She's all right, but naturally she loved her own small children more than the two of us left over from the previous marriages, and being a bit stupid and not very pretty she was determined that at least she'd rule the roost. I didn't feel really happy in Lappesheim after she came.

Anyway, the whole place would be too small for me in the long run. I'd far rather live in a city. You're not supposed to say that kind of thing these days, on account of World Outlook and the government. Right-thinking people don't prefer cities or think they're nicer than the countryside. And all the poets nowadays write things saying the only kind of Nature you must love is your original natural background. They keep building bigger and bigger cities all the same, and laying main roads over the redolent soil. The point of the redolent soil is that poets have to sing its praises so as to avoid thinking any stupid thoughts, like what is going on in our cities, and what's happening to the people. You also need the redolent soil for making films about country life which the public do not flock to see. Heini once explained all this to me and Liska. Liska is in love with Heini. I don't always understand him myself, but that doesn't make *me* fall in love with him.

Anyway, I don't think the provincial governors, the Gauleiters, and high-up Ministers would much fancy spending the winter in Lappesheim, when the Mosel's full of poisonous-looking yellow mud, and mist weighs down on the whole valley so thick you can hardly breathe. It's always dark, and you stumble over holes in the roads. The only way to stand it is if you have some kind of business of your own, and you're always thinking how to improve it. Or if you have a husband and children to annoy you, which at least is better than being bored to death. I don't want to spend my life there, and neither does Algin, though he carries on in the stories he writes these days as if a right-thinking person ought to clasp every cowpat to his breast.

When I was sixteen, I went to live with Aunt Adelheid in Cologne. She has a stationer's shop there, in Friesen Street. She's my dead mother's sister, and it was my mother who let her have the money for the shop. Aunt Adelheid either has to pay me back some of that money every month or let me live with her free. This was another reason for Aunt Adelheid to dislike me. I'd never have stuck it out there as long as I did – two whole years – but for her son Franz. It is hard to believe he's her son; she doesn't love him, either. I helped Aunt Adelheid in the shop. I love selling things, and everyone says I have a gift for getting on with customers.

When the Führer came to power, Aunt Adelheid went all political, and put up pictures of him, bought swastika flags and joined the National Socialist Women's Club, where she got to meet a good class of person as a German wife and mother.

Then there was air raid drill, held in what used to be the Young Men's Christian Association hall. Aunt Adelheid went regularly, taking me along, and she made sure everyone else in the building went too and didn't wriggle out of it. She was nearly the death of frail old Herr Pütz, who lives on the top floor.

Old Pütz is a pensioner, leading a quiet, peaceful life on his own. He has nicely brushed white hair and walks with neat, tottery little footsteps. Aunt Adelheid made him come to air raid drill. That day we had to put on gas masks, which practically smothered you, and then run up a staircase. Old Pütz stood in a dark corner, all shaky, holding the gas mask in his thin little hands and no doubt hoping nobody would notice him. But Aunt Adelheid's beady black eyes noticed him all right. He had to put his gas mask on, and Aunt Adelheid chased him up the staircase ahead of her. Up in the loft he collapsed. Everyone was horrified, though you could only tell from their fluttering hands and agitated footsteps, because there were no human faces in sight, just hideous masks. Pütz's crumpled body lay there on the floor in his one good, dark blue Sunday suit, and we could hear him breathing stertorously inside his mask. Aunt Adelheid had put the mask on him wrong, and it was difficult getting his head out again. I thought he was going to die, but he recovered, very slowly. It was like a miracle.

'Pütz,' said Aunt Adelheid, 'I hope you realize you should be thankful to me? But for me you'd have been done for in a moment of serious danger.' 'Just let me die in my bed,' Pütz whimpered in a voice like a mouse's squeak, 'just let me die in my bed.' 'Pütz,' said Aunt Adelheid sternly, 'you have failed to understand the new Germany. You have failed to understand the Führer's will for reconstruction. Old folk like you must be either ignored or forced to see where their welfare lies!' Later on, Aunt Adelheid campaigned successfully to be made warden of the building. That means that if there's a genuine air raid she gets a gun, and everyone in the building is under her orders. And she has the right to shoot anyone who disobeys her.

A thousand enemy aircraft wouldn't frighten me as much as Aunt Adelheid with a gun and the power to give orders. There will be no need for any enemy airman to drop a bomb on Aunt Adelheid's building in order to kill the people inside, because Aunt Adelheid will do the job for him in advance. Unless Schauwecker murders her first, that is. He's another enthusiastic Nazi, and lives on the first floor. He looks like a great fat, yellow sponge, and he is stage manager at the City Theatre. He used to be a member of some sort of organization which got him his job. Then he was going to be sacked, because he was always feeling up the actresses with walk-on parts – he was in charge of them, and could go into their dressing-room – and doing really disgusting things, and he wouldn't even leave children alone. I know him; he's an old pig. I was always afraid of meeting him out in the street at night on my own. He wasn't sacked, just given a warning. But on account of all he'd suffered he became an anti-Semite.

He has a tearful wife, and three children who are all in the Hitler Youth movement. He's much respected in the Party because he knows a whole lot about the actors and the other people working at the theatre. And *he* was dead set on being warden of the building, and he would have been too, but for

Aunt Adelheid. However, Aunt Adelheid had witnesses to the fact that when a man came round selling lottery tickets in aid of the Winter Relief programme, he had said, behind the man's back, 'I've no intention of buying any of that fool's trash.' This amounted to sabotage of the Winter Relief effort, and Aunt Adelheid had only to inform on him, so she was well able to scare Schauwecker into letting her be warden. He'll get his own back when the war comes and everything's in confusion.

Then Aunt Adelheid did something really horrible, something which might have been the death of *me*. After that I wasn't going to stay on at her place, and I went to Algin in Frankfurt. He'd been to see me in Cologne, and he'd always been nice to me. Thank goodness he was glad to have me, and I stayed.

Algin's been all over the place, even Berlin, where he wrote for the newspapers. Then he began writing books, and one day he became really famous. There were reviews of his books in all the papers. They're novels. One is about a woman who steals things from a department store, but she's a good person all the same, it was just that there wasn't anything else she could do. She gets badly treated by one man, he's a cashier, and then she has an affair with a waiter, but that doesn't turn out well either.

Algin used to send copies of his books to Lappesheim, and we looked at them, too. When November came and the vintage was over and the tourists had gone home, my father used to read half a page every evening. But I don't think he ever got to the end of any of the books.

They even made a film of one of Algin's books, and it was shown in Koblenz. Father and I and six other people from the village went to Koblenz specially to see it. When we were in the cinema we felt just as if the place belonged to Algin, and all the film actors too, and he was responsible for the whole thing. Even the little torches the usherettes carried. The posters outside said, in big, bold letters, '*Shadows Without Sun*. From the celebrated novel by Algin Moder.' We never really stopped to think if we liked the film, we just felt pleased and very proud, particularly my father. He didn't say anything, but you could tell how proud he was because he took us all into the Königsbacher Bar afterwards and spent quite a lot of money.

After that he put the book on the little table by the counter in the pub, where he always puts the newspapers, so that his customers could see it. There was an article about Algin in one newspaper, with a photograph of him, and Father had it handsomely and expensively framed and hung it over the settle in the bar.

Algin sent home suits and dresses, and woollen waistcoats and expensive cognac for Father, who knows a thing or two about liquor. Father sent Algin the biggest salmon he caught in the Eltzbach, and the best vintage years of our wine. All the villagers envied us Algin, and the old Forest Supervisor went so far as to tell Father, 'Moder, you should be a proud man! Your son's made good.' Perhaps my father would have been even prouder if Algin had made good as a general, Father himself being a veteran of the Stahlhelm corps, but obviously the times just weren't right for Algin to get to be a general.

So my father had to content himself with the splendid things the newspapers printed about Algin, all down there in black and white. He *was* content, too, and proud. He even made some sharpish remarks about Father Bender, the only person in the village who had read Algin's book, and who said that when God had endowed Algin richly with gifts and talents it was poor thanks to Him to deny the giver of such gifts.

Father Bender's in protective custody now, for thrashing the parish council chairman's son because the parish council chairman's son made use of the church wall instead of a tree or a lavatory. The boy is high up in the Hitler Youth, and as well as being parish council chairman his father's an old campaigner, and used to lead a detachment.

Algin's book is not on the little table by the counter any more, because the National Socialists put it on a black list. Its trouble is that it's demoralizing and offends against the basic will for reconstruction of the Third Reich. That's what they said in the Nazi newspaper in Koblenz. My father wasn't a National Socialist to start with, but he was all for a basic will for reconstruction.

Also, he had to think of his customers, so he hung a picture of the Führer over the settle instead of the framed article about Algin. It annoyed my father to think of Algin writing banned books, after he'd laid out good money on his education. After all, said my father, you have to show respect for the Führer, and the national emblem, and if Segebrecht, who keeps another local pub, has landed himself in a concentration camp then it's entirely his own fault. Segebrecht can certainly carry an amazing amount of drink, but he *will* keep putting it back, and it was one day when he was drunk that he painted a swastika on his lavatory floor. When Pitter Lambert came into the bar and asked what the idea was, he shouted at the top of his voice, 'To show all the arseholes what they've gone and elected, that's the idea.' Well, no good's going to come of that kind of thing.

Anyway, Algin *had* made good, as everyone had to admit. I used to think it must be wonderful, and I'd have loved to be brilliant and successful too, but now I wouldn't really, not any more, because things can go wrong so quickly, and you never get much fun out of any of it in the long run, either.

When Algin was first famous he thought he'd go up in the world a bit, and he did, and now it's a burden to him, one he can't shake off. Since the new government banned one of Algin's books, he has to be scrupulously careful what he writes, and he doesn't earn much money any more. His entire life, his whole working day from morning to night, is spent making enough to pay for his apartment and the furniture. Because when he was first famous he rented an apartment with lovely big rooms on the main Bockenheim Road, where the most prosperous people in Frankfurt have always lived, and lovely lush magnolia trees bloom in the front gardens in spring.

Then Algin married Liska, because she's so tall and lovely that even women who don't like her say she really is quite something. He also married her because she admired his divine gift for language, and because you need a wife as well as an apartment if you're going up in the world. They furnished the apartment with expensive rugs and cushions, and furniture which is so low it makes you feel somebody sawed the legs off the chairs and tables one cold winter and fed them into the stove. Although the apartment has central heating. Alcoves have been built into some of the walls for books. Algin saw this apartment as a magnificent stage setting for a theatrical show performed by himself. He wanted people to come and applaud, and be aware that Algin was playing a leading part.

Algin isn't happy any more. Liska isn't happy any more. I love them both. When I came here they gave me board and lodging just like that, and now I'm running the household for them. All Liska can do about the house is create chaos and stuffed toy animals. She used to work with handicrafts in Berlin, and she still does. It even earns her a little money. Her soft toys are silly, daft – but amusing and appealing too.

Oh dear, now Herr Kulmbach's ordering yet another round of kirsch. And I've got an incredible amount of work to do tomorrow, because tomorrow evening is Liska's big party.

Gerti called for me at noon today, because she was going to buy a pink blouse and wanted me to come along to the shops and tell her which suited her best. Even Liska says I have good taste in clothes, and people are always wanting me to knit them sweaters. Actually I can knit fast, and well. If I really do marry Franz, I can always earn us a little money by knitting. However, here in Frankfurt I've been moving in circles which are quite different from anything Franz is used to. I mix with high-class, rich, intelligent people here. Franz wouldn't know what to say to them.

Well, anyway, we were out in search of a blouse, Gerti and myself. We looked in Goethe Street and the Zeil. Then Gerti said why didn't we go and have a coffee in the café in the Rossmarkt, so we did. Jews sometimes use this café, because unlike nearly all other bars and restaurants, it doesn't have a notice up saying *Jews Not Welcome*.

The better class of Jews mostly stay at home anyway. If they do want to go out in public there are still three cafés in Frankfurt they can visit. These happen to be the three best cafés, which is hard luck on Aryans, who are afraid of going there too, with good reason. The good reason is that the Nazi paper, the *Stürmer*, will write about them if they do and call them lackeys of the Jews. And if they have official positions they get sacked. Only a very few brave Aryans dare go in, people without jobs to lose.

Similarly, a few brave Jews venture into the Rossmarkt café.
They drink light beer which they don't really like, so as to look
inconspicuous and Aryan. Whereas in this particular café Aryans
don't happen to drink beer.

Gerti said why didn't we have a vermouth with our coffee,
and then another one, and I was her guest. She kept looking at
the door. Her neck must have hurt from all that turning to look.
She was hoping Dieter Aaron would come in.

Goodness knows how often I've told her, 'Gerti, don't make
yourself and Dieter unhappy.' Dieter is what they call a person
of mixed race, first class or maybe third class – I can never get
the hang of these labels. But anyway, Gerti's not supposed to
have anything to do with him because of the race laws. If all
Gerti does is simply sit in the corner of a café with Dieter,
holding hands, they can get punished severely for offending
against national feeling. Still, what does a girl care about the law
when she wants a man? And if a man wants a girl, it's all the
same to him if the executioner's standing right behind him with
his axe, so long as he gets one thing. Once he's had it, of course,
it is not all the same to him any more.

I don't mean that Dieter Aaron is a totally unacceptable sort
of mixed-race person. He's polite, and nice, and young, with soft,
brown, round, velvety eyes. He's never been very energetic or
competent, and his father has never been happy about him.
Old Aaron *is* very competent, and rich, and he has a fine,
grandly-decorated detached house with a garage. He sells curtains and furnishing fabrics abroad. Gerti says it's an export
business, and Jews can run export businesses; they aren't
banned. So old Aaron has no problems with his business although
he is a full Jew. However, he doesn't like people to call him a
Jew. He says he's not a Jew, he's a non-Aryan.

I've sometimes been invited to the Aarons' with Algin and
Liska, and Algin almost always quarrels with the old man.
Because Algin is against the National Socialists and old Aaron
isn't. Old Aaron thinks the Nazis have put the German mentality
in order and saved him from the Communists, who would have
taken away all he has. He never has any trouble in big, grand
hotels; indeed, he gets excellent treatment, and they even offer

him a chair at the Revenue offices. There are some very inferior riffraff among the Jews, he says, so he can understand anti-Semitism, and as for the armed forces, there are some fine fellows among *them*, it's a pleasure to look at them. Frau Aaron is not Jewish. She is dry and hard as old straw, and she dominates her husband. Young Aaron is of mixed race because of his non-Jewish mother, who loves him so madly it's practically indecent.

Dieter is in love with Gerti, but he's scared stiff of his mother. He used to work in a chemicals factory, a job obtained by much effort and expense on his father's part, but now he can't do it any more. Nobody knows what will become of him. For the time being, he drives his father to business meetings and takes the Dobermann out for walks. He also goes looking for Gerti, and she goes looking for him.

And then the pair of them sit in a bar looking at each other, the air around them positively quivering with lovesickness. Everyone in the bar must notice; no good can come of it. They just live for the moment, and cause the air to quiver, and don't stop to wonder what next. Gerti thinks the good Lord will help them, because she's so beautiful, and the good Lord is a man. Dieter thinks, by turns, what his mother thinks and what Gerti thinks. Also, he is afraid of his father.

Sometimes Gerti and Dieter do try to plan for the future, but then they look into each other's eyes, and all thought fades away. Sometimes I keep them company, so that the impression they make in the bar won't be quite so dangerous. I don't like doing this, and I always feel very foolish. I could weep with the worry of it. They're both so pretty and so nice, and they may be hauled off to jail tomorrow. Why are they so crazy? I can't understand it. Other people dance, but they can't. The radio is playing string music, soft as a feather bed. Bright light shimmers in the wine. The wine is sour, but they are drinking hot, bright radiance. I long for Franz, and Gerti's voice grows thin and faltering. The proprietor of the place keeps glancing at us – perhaps he knows Gerti from her parents' shop and he'll inform on her tomorrow. Dieter's well known in Frankfurt too, through his father. There are people wearing Party badges at the next table – oh, dear God, we must get out of here! We must find another bar, and yet another, and some time disaster will strike.

Perhaps the two of them wouldn't love each other so much if they were allowed to. However, there's nothing more idiotic than wondering why people love each other when they *are* in love.

So when Gerti and I were sitting in the Rossmarkt café this afternoon, she thought Dieter might turn up because she'd been there with him once or twice, around this time in the afternoon. They hadn't made a date. All the same, Gerti was nearly weeping with fury because Dieter didn't come in. Now she won't see him again until tomorrow, at Liska's party; the Aarons are invited. And then they will have to be very careful, because of the old Aarons and because of Betty Raff. And I'm not sure that all the other guests are entirely safe, either.

Gerti wanted to have one more vermouth. She suddenly looked dead and drained. The way a woman looks when she's been waiting with all her might, waiting and longing, and all for nothing. Gerti did not want to buy a pink blouse any more, and anyway there wouldn't have been enough money left. We decided to go home without the blouse. It was five in the afternoon. There was turmoil around the Opera House. People, and swastika flags, and garlands of fir, and SS men. The place was in confusion, all excited preparations, much like preparations for the handing out of Christmas presents in a prosperous family with quantities of children. You get used to feverish celebrations of something or other going on all the time in Germany, so that you often don't stop to ask what it is this time, why all the fuss and the garlands and the flags?

Suddenly we felt cold. We were in a hurry to get home. But the SS wouldn't let us cross the Opera House Square to get to the Bockenheim Road. We asked why not; what was going on? But the SS are always arrogant and inclined to put on airs. This lot had nothing better to do than stand around, but they still couldn't find time to answer us. Possibly their minds were working away so frantically that they could only manage to give a contemptuous shrug of their military shoulders.

Gerti's eyes went dark as coal with rage. I know her in that mood: it makes her dangerous, and then of course she's the greatest danger of all to herself. So I asked one of the SS men again, sweet as sugar, very humbly, as if I thought he was one of the greatest rulers of Germany – well, that's the way men like a girl to treat them.

So then the SS man said the Führer would be coming down the Mainz Road to the Opera House at eight. If we wanted to get to the other side of the square we'd have to go round. Yes, of course the Führer was coming! How could I have forgotten? After all, little Berta Silias was due to break through the crowd with flowers, and Frau Silias had talked of nothing else for days.

It was beginning to rain. People were gathering in the square, more and more of them all the time. It looked quite dangerous, as if they'd crush each other to death. Everyone wanted to see something, some of them may not even have known what there would be to see, but all the same they were risking their lives.

Possibly the Führer thought, afterwards, that the people had come flocking up out of love for him. No, being the Führer he'll be too clever to think that. Thousands more people join the carnival parade in Cologne, and clamber up on lampposts and high rooftops, breaking arms, legs, anything – they don't mind. It's just a kind of sport: they're proud to have got a good viewpoint, so they can say, and believe, they were in the carnival. And classy people always want to have been at something classy – like Press balls and first nights. But as those things cost a lot of money, there isn't usually such a dangerous crush as in the enormous crowds of people who don't have any money and can only go to shows that don't cost them anything.

We reached the Mainz Road. It was officially lined the whole way down by SA men, who always look broader than usual on these important occasions. Mostly they don't have anything much to do these days, and go about looking as if they've shrunk a bit. Kurt Pielmann and Herr Kulmbach, for instance, resent the fact that there isn't a campaign on any more. Today, however, they could form an imposing cordon, which puts new life into them.

A thin, grey man with a bicycle was going on angrily about

not being allowed through. He had finally got a new job, he said, and he had to be on time. Unpunctuality could mean bad trouble for him. And even if his employers did realize he couldn't help being late, they might still be angry with him. Life's nearly always like that: you put difficulties in a person's way, and a slight aura of something dubious and unpleasant still clings to him whether it is his fault or not. 'Look, be reasonable, will you?' a fairly high-up SA man, drinking coffee from his flask, told the thin, grey cyclist. 'Don't bleat on like that! Just you be thankful to the Führer for his high ideals!'

'That's right,' said the thin, grey man, 'the Führer gets to have the ideals and we get to carry the can.' His voice was trembling; you could tell his nerves were worn to a shred. The people who'd heard him were struck dumb with alarm, and the SA man went red in the face and could scarcely get his breath back. All at once the grey man looked utterly broken, extinguished. Three SA men led him away. He didn't put up a struggle.

His bicycle was lying on the ground. People stood around it in a circle, staring in nervous silence. It shone dully in the rain, and had a subversive look about it; nobody dared touch it. Then a fat woman made an angry face, flung her arm up in the air in the salute of the Führer, said, 'Disgusting!' and kicked the bicycle. Several other women kicked it too. And then the cordon opened and let us through.

The Esplanade café is diagonally opposite the Opera House. It has pansies flowering outside it in summer time, and its customers are nearly all Jews. Gerti and I ought to have gone on down the Bockenheim Road, but there was a cordon blocking that road off too, so we went into the Esplanade. The first thing I did was phone Liska, who said that was all right, she'd make a bite of supper, and Betty Raff could lend a hand too. Gerti rang her mother. Her mother said Kurt Pielmann had come from Würzburg and would be meeting her in the Henninger Bar about nine this evening.

Kurt Pielmann's in love with Gerti and wants to marry her. His father has put a lot of money into Gerti's parents' shop. If he takes it out now, the business will fail. You can't help understanding them and seeing their point. I persuaded Gerti to keep the date with Kurt Pielmann. She can be friendly to him, after all; that doesn't mean she has to marry him, and she certainly does not, *not* have to kiss him. With a man like that, all she has to do is say she's glad there are people like him around, and she'd like him to tell her about National Socialism and introduce her to a wonderful world of ideas. And she isn't mature enough yet to be the lifelong companion of a National Socialist and old campaigner, but she would like to improve her mind until she is, and the way he can help her is by sending her constructive literature. The likes of Kurt Pielmann will be sure to send her the constructive literature, if only because then he can believe he's read it himself. I know about this sort of thing through my father, and Aunt Adelheid, and a good many other people too. They find reading far too much of a strain, far too boring. You can bet your sweet life they haven't read *Mein Kampf* from beginning to end yet. Not that I have either. But they've bought it, and glanced at it now and again, and in the end they believe they've read the whole thing.

Heini once said, 'People either buy a book and don't read it. Or they borrow a book and don't give it back, and still don't read it. Or they give it back without reading it. But they've heard so much about the book, and gone to all that trouble buying it or remembering to return it, they really do feel they know it inside out. So they're familiar with the book without ever having read it.' This way, he said, thousands of Germans had read Goethe and Nietzsche and other poets and philosophers without going to the bother of really reading them. Look at it like that, and our Führer has something in common with Goethe.

Gerti and I sat in the Esplanade while the place got emptier and emptier around us, quite deserted. All the Jews were leaving. Speeches came roaring out of the loudspeaker like a storm. The café was full of them: speeches about the Führer who would soon be here, about a free Germany, and about the enthusiasm of the crowd. Two elderly ladies came in, thin and neat, looking like spinsters of slender means, maybe small-town schoolteachers on a visit to the city. They ordered coffee and apple tart with cream. Just as they were about to start eating, the Horst Wessel Song came over the radio. The old ladies put their spoons down, stood up and raised their arms. You have to do that, because you never know who may be watching, who may denounce you. Perhaps they were afraid of each other. Gerti and I stood up too.

The radio fell silent for a moment. A waiter came over and asked Gerti if she wanted to see it all from a balcony. Since we were stuck there, of course we did want. We went up and down in the lift with the waiter; all the balconies were crammed full of people. But in the end the waiter found a balcony where he could squeeze us in. He wasn't interested in seeing anything himself.

I was half sitting on a fat man's lap; I couldn't make his face out properly, but his breath was like a greasy, smelly ball that kept flying into my face. There were elegant ladies and gentlemen sitting behind us, keeping still and paying attention as if they were in a box at the theatre. Gerti herself said she felt as if we'd been given free seats for a show, only we didn't really fit in, and we weren't dressed for the occasion.

Over to the right of the Opera House Square, where it's almost like a park, a black sea of people had gathered, moving back and forth in slow waves. A dull sort of light shone over them. Several SS men were bustling about the cleared square in an excited manner, frantically waving their arms about. But still nothing happened.

Now and then SS men carried fainting women out of the sea of people, so the wait wasn't too boring for the spectators in the balconies.

Then, suddenly, cars came down the road – fast and quiet as downy feathers flying. And so beautiful, too! I never saw such cars in my life before. So many of them as well, so many of them! All the Gauleiters, and high-up Party men accompanying them, drove up in those cars; it was splendid. They must all be enormously rich. When I think of Franz, and I imagine him living for a hundred years working from morning to night – always supposing he *had* work – and not drinking or smoking all that hundred years, doing nothing but save, save, save – well, I work it out that even in a hundred years he still couldn't buy a car like that. Maybe in a thousand years. But who lives to be a thousand years old?

I enjoyed seeing the beautiful cars; they looked like marvellous, shiny, racing beetles seen from above. And all the people down below, who must have been worn out with waiting by now, were enjoying themselves too, because something was finally happening, although only the people at the front of the crowd could see any of it.

Shouts arose in the distance. *Heil* Hitler! The roar of the crowd came surging up, closer and closer, up to our balcony – widespread, hoarse, a little weary. And a car drove slowly past with the Führer standing in it, like Prince Carnival in the carnival parade. But he wasn't as funny and cheerful as Prince Carnival, and he wasn't throwing sweets and nosegays, just raising an empty hand.

A little sky-blue ball came rolling out of the dark ranks of the crowd and into the street, making for the car. It was little Berta Silias, who'd been chosen to break through the crowd, because the Führer often likes to be photographed with children. But he can't have felt like it this time. Berta was left standing there, a solitary little speck with a huge bouquet of flowers.

The Führer had passed. Some SS men were kneeling round little Berta, lights were flashing, photographs were being taken. Well, Berta may get into the paper after all, even if it's only with some SS men and not the Führer. That will be some small consolation to Frau Silias.

Men who were currently famous were getting into position on the long balcony of the Opera House, with much ceremony, bowing politely to each other. They waved to the crowd too.

They weren't really doing anything of interest, but you were allowed to look at them.

Gerti's opinion was that you didn't get much fun out of looking at these eminent men, the eminent men must get far more fun out of having all of *us* looking at *them*.

On the other hand, there were ladies on our balcony in ecstasies because they could recognize one General Blomberg, and Göring too, because Göring had a touch of red on his jacket, and we all know from photographs that he likes to wear stylish suits. Though by now he's really so well known he doesn't need to make his mark by wearing striking clothes.

Algin sometimes has a visitor, a young actor who can't get parts, who has to make a good impression by his appearance, so he wears very expensive ties, and pigskin gloves so bright you can see them a mile off. But Göring already *has* a part, in his own way. Then again, however, even established film stars can never let up – they have to keep showing their public the latest thing in fashion and elegance. I expect someone like Göring is obliged to think hard all the time, if he's going to keep offering the German people something new. And men like that have to find time to govern the country as well. Personally, I can't think how they do it all. Take the Führer: he devotes almost his entire life to being photographed for his people. Just imagine, what an achievement! Having your picture taken the whole time with children and pet dogs, indoors and out of doors – never any rest. *And* constantly going about in aeroplanes, or sitting through long Wagner operas, because that's German art, and he sacrifices himself for German art as well.

Well, fame always demands some sacrifices. I read that once in an article about Marlene Dietrich. They say the Führer eats nothing but radishes and rye bread with cheese spread. That's another sacrifice to fame. Hollywood film actresses sometimes eat even less, because they mustn't get fat. And they don't drink or smoke either, so as to keep their looks. Liska sometimes diets till she's quite ill, just to lose weight.

I can well imagine our Führer wanting to have a particularly slim, handsome figure, what with being photographed all the time and appearing in newsreels and Party Congress films. And maybe he'd like to show up well in contrast to Göring, and Dr Ley, and a number of other ministers and mayors, who have all got noticeably fatter. You can see that any day from their pictures in magazines.

Anyway, there were these eminent men in the flesh, standing on the Opera House balcony. The balcony, with them on it, was illuminated; everywhere else was dark. The lights in the square had been turned off so that the Army would show to good effect. The Reichswehr men wore shiny steel helmets, and they were carrying blazing torches. They did a sort of ballet dance with these torches, to the sound of a military band. It was a tattoo, and also a historic moment, and it looked very pretty.

The world was big and dark blue, the dancing men were black, moving all together – faceless, silent, dark figures all in time. I once saw some African war dances in an educational film. The African dances were rather livelier, but I did like the Reichswehr's dance very much too.

TWO

The crowd had dispersed, the eminent men had gone gliding away in their magical cars, the Army had marched off to the sound of the band. One abandoned torch lay smouldering on the ground, a faint glow in the dark night. Nobody trod it out.

The street lights were turned on, and you could see again.

Gerti and I ran into Kurt Pielmann right outside the Henninger Bar. He was in his SA uniform and a state of great excitement. It had been wonderful, he said, had we seen everything, couldn't he just do with a glass of beer!

He made Gerti sit down beside him almost forcibly, so that everyone in the bar would think she was his property. The place was getting fuller all the time. People always feel like a beer after something exciting. Big, fat Herr Kulmbach came in, sweating, all red and bloated, and asked if he could join us at our table, because he wanted company to discuss today's events. We know him because he's a waiter in the 'Squirrel', where we go quite often: I mean Algin, Gerti, Liska, and some other people we know.

When we go there, Herr Kulmbach always gives us the best seats, and altogether he is really very nice. He's seen the Führer four times already, but he never tires of seeing him again.

Kulmbach's parents have a small public house in the Taunus which the Führer used to patronize years ago. Kulmbach often tells us about it. His story is always slightly different, and the Führer's visits have increased and multiplied at each re-telling. After a while you get to feel the Führer spent half his life in the Kulmbachs' pub and couldn't live without Herr Kulmbach, just as Herr Kulmbach can't live without him. There's no telling how much of this Kulmbach is actually making up. He's an honest man at heart, and never short-changes you when you're paying

your bill. He's an old campaigner too, and means to stay that
way.

He went to the Party Rally in Nuremberg last year, and had
a uniform and jackboots made specially for the occasion, at his
own expense. He's paying for them on hire purchase. That trip
to the Nuremberg Party Rally was the greatest experience of
his life, he says, he could spend hours telling you about it.
Though all he actually does tell you is that the earth shook during
the firework display, it literally shook. Yes, I'd have thought
that was exciting too.

And now Gerti has to go picking a quarrel with Kurt Pielmann
in the most dangerous possible way, in front of fanatically
National Socialist Kulmbach, of all people. Pielmann was so
pleased with the Reichswehr a moment ago, and now Gerti is
tormenting him by telling him she thinks they look better than
the Stormtroopers. Of course Pielmann immediately says Gerti
hasn't got the ideological point of the Nazi World Outlook. This
is what Party members always say when they're annoyed. Gerti
says right, she'd like him to explain the ideological point of the
World Outlook. To which, of course, Kurt Pielmann says that if
Gerti hasn't got the point by now it's no use explaining. Gerti
and I have learnt from experience that this sort of subject only
lands us in trouble.

Kulmbach, sounding perfectly friendly, says it's all a matter
of the Führer's personality. You only have to look into his eyes.
What's more, the Führer always does what he says he'll do.
And look at the way he sacrifices himself in his speeches!
Goebbels's speeches may be wonderfully keen and intellectual,
but it's the Führer who makes the emotional sacrifices.

I kick Gerti under the table, but still she won't shut up. She
says didn't the Führer once say all Jews smell of garlic? What
she'd like to know is just how many Jews the Führer has actually
smelt, that's all. If you think a person is revolting, well, you
don't keep getting close enough to smell him. The Jews *she*
knows don't smell, anyway, and as for garlic, she is very fond
of eating it herself. This upsets Pielmann no end. If Gerti can
talk like that, he says, she is racially contaminated. Kulmbach
tries to calm Pielmann down, saying he himself once knew a Jew

who was a decent sort of fellow, and then he orders another round of kirsch.

At this point, thank heavens, I've managed to get Gerti to come to the Ladies with me.

One of the SS men from the next table followed us and asked, very politely, if Gerti could come and have a beer with him somewhere else, later, or if she was booked up for the whole evening, and maybe I'd like to come along as well, his friend would make up the party. Oh, come on, no need for us to be so chilly and off-putting! Had we seen the tattoo today? The SS man never took his eyes off Gerti. Unfortunately he didn't look as smart as SS men usually do, because the SS have had a good deal of effort and exertion recently. When our troops moved into the Rhineland, they had to be on constant alert; we were expecting enemy aircraft any moment, and never thought the French would take it all so meekly. The French are an underhand lot, and might have been expected to defend themselves. We didn't feel at all happy about it. But it was what the Führer wanted: he ordered in the troops, putting all of us ordinary folk in deadly danger almost without our knowing it. Perhaps we're still in danger.

I mean, it's pure chance that poison gas isn't eating my body away right now. The Führer doesn't mind taking risks. He can say the word and declare war tomorrow, and kill the lot of us. We're all in his hands.

The SS man's expression was grave and soothing, as if he'd saved us from something and would in all circumstances go on saving us. When he stopped talking for a moment, Gerti instantly did another frightful thing, just to get rid of him. She has this awful urge to be unpleasant to Nazis and annoy them. She told the SS man she was afraid she couldn't date him because she was Jewish. Which is not true, and Gerti only said it out of fury, and contrariness, and what she'd had to drink. Of course the SS man immediately looked at us with chilly dislike. 'Why didn't you say so before, then?' he asked. Though he hadn't let us get a word in edgeways. So Gerti suggested he should consult his Aryan blood and ask it why it hadn't spoken up to tell him, the way Aryan blood is supposed to do. To stop the whole situation getting mortally dangerous, I said quickly, 'My friend was only joking – your feelings were quite right first time, of course, and she isn't Jewish, but she's with her boyfriend this evening. He's a Stormtrooper.' At which the SS man clicked heels in an exceedingly injured manner. 'One does not joke about such things,' he said.

Once I had Gerti safe in the Ladies, I told her she might well ruin herself and her whole family, meddling with politics in that pointless way, and we could only hope Kulmbach would calm Kurt Pielmann down. And Gerti had better tell Kurt Pielmann she'd just turned an invitation from an SS man down flat, even indignantly – there's no better way of conciliating an SA man, because the Brownshirts all resent the superior attitude of the SS; the general public think they're classy, being the Führer's bodyguard. But nowadays the Regular Army men of the Reichswehr are considered the classiest and most superior of all, so the SS, in their turn, resent *them*.

Herr Kulmbach had been saying the Führer had united the whole German nation. Which is true enough, it's just that the people making up the whole German nation don't get on with each other. But that doesn't make any difference to political unity, I suppose.

The Ladies of the Henninger Bar consists of three separate cubicles, one of them a broom cupboard. Gerti and I looked inside them to make sure there was no one to overhear us.

It always used to be so cosy when two girls went to the Ladies together. You powdered your noses, and exchanged rapid but important information about men and love. And you combed your hair, and the pair of you wondered whether to let the men you were with take you home, and if they'd get above themselves, and want to kiss when you didn't. Or if you did, you'd be terribly worried the man might not think you pretty enough. You exchanged excited advice in the Ladies. It was often silly advice, but still, conversations in the Ladies were fun, and interesting.

But politics is in the air even in the Ladies these days. Gerti says she supposes it's something if you find one without a lavatory attendant who expects you to say '*Heil* Hitler' and wants ten pfennigs into the bargain.

And now, suddenly, Gerti is weeping bitterly, because she didn't see Dieter Aaron today, so I have to comfort her. Why does a girl like Gerti have to go falling in love with a banned person of mixed race, for goodness' sake, when there are plenty of men around the authorities *would* let her love? It's hard enough to know your way around all the rules the authorities lay down for business – business, as we all know, can be very trickily organized – and now we have to know the rules for love too. It isn't easy, it really isn't. Before you know it, you may find yourself castrated or in prison, which is not pleasant. Love is supposed to be all right, and German women are supposed to have children, but before you can do that some kind of process involving feelings is called for. And the law says no mistakes must be made in this process. I suppose the safest thing is not to love anyone at all. For as long as *that's* allowed.

Gerti is washing her swollen eyes. We must go back to our table. My head's full of confused, random thoughts, like a ball of wool I must knit into words. I must knit a stocking of words. It takes so long, and I forget what I was going to say a minute ago, as if I'd dropped a stitch.

Oh lord, here comes Frau Breitwehr. Was she in the bar too? '*Heil* Hitler, Frau Breitwehr!'

She has a grocer's shop in Liebig Street. Her hair looks dusty, and she is fat and highly strung. When she wears a hat it always looks as if it's on crooked, even when she's put it on straight. We're good customers of hers: we go to her shop for cognac and oranges and canned prawns. Algin loves prawns for breakfast. They make him feel he's abroad.

When Frau Breitwehr is in her shop she's quite alarming. She is brisk and stern with her customers, and she has three assistants who are terrified of her, although they're not well paid. But when Frau Breitwehr goes out, there is something about her makes you feel sorry for her, the way you'd feel sorry for a bird that fell out of its nest in the rain. Yet she wears a genuine silver fox fur. It doesn't make her look beautiful, but she went to great lengths to acquire it.

Everyone in the street knows Frau Breitwehr had always dreamed of owning a silver fox fur, and she asked her husband to give her one for Christmas. Her husband is small and afraid of her, but sometimes she's afraid of him too, because in an odd way fear is always mutual. He said he *would* give her a silver fox fur for Christmas, but then, instead, he gave her a washing machine which cost much more. He was afraid his wife might come to consider the silver fox fur a frivolous expense, in time.

So then Frau Breitwehr began putting money out of the till aside, on the sly, for whatever happened her husband mustn't know of it.

When she'd siphoned off enough cash like this, she asked Frau Silias, whose husband is an Honorary Administrator, to come into the shop when Herr Breitwehr was serving behind the counter. Frau Silias's instructions were to pretend she had a cheap old fake silver fox fur she was going to sell. She was to offer it to Frau Breitwehr as part payment of the account she'd run up at the shop. We know all this from Frau Silias, who is a neighbour of ours, and can't exist without telling everything she knows to everyone she meets in the street, daily.

Herr Silias got to be an Honorary Administrator quite recently, and also warden of our block of buildings. All this is a source of pride and joy to an ambitious man, but doesn't bring in much money. Herr Silias's job is with the municipal health insurance organization. But now he has so much honorary unpaid work to do, his salary won't stretch to the standard of living he requires. For instance, he likes bottled Würzburg beer for his supper, and plenty of best cured pork, to help him feel like a campaigner and a member of the movement. He needs to feel like this all the more because he didn't join the Party until the last moment, after the Nazis came to power, though no one is supposed to know that.

His wife has to get him the cured pork and bottled beer – after all, what are wives for? – and so Frau Silias ran up quite a bill at the Breitwehrs' shop, because she thinks her husband and the movement are both heroic. So she wants him to have everything he'd like, even though he doesn't bring her much home in the way of salary, having many expenses in his official position. And thus Frau Silias, wife of the Honorary Administrator, was in debt to Frau Breitwehr of the grocery shop. The two of them were obliged to help each other anyway, both being in the National Socialist Women's Club, where you have to fight together and think of the common good, and feel the bond of your true German nature, and show it in deeds and folk-dancing.

Herr Breitwehr believed Frau Silias's story about the fake silver fox fur. So then Frau Breitwehr went off to Godenheimer's the furriers, even though it's a Jewish shop and a good German woman is not supposed to buy anything from Jews. But Godenheimer's had the best and cheapest silver foxes, and buttered Frau Breitwehr up, and called her 'Madam' every other sentence. So she bought the silver fox fur. When she wears it, they look like a rich fur taking a poor woman out for a walk.

And now Frau Breitwehr is washing her hands in the Ladies and looking at Gerti with interest, because it is still obvious that Gerti has been crying. Frau Breitwehr says they are sitting over in a corner at the back of the bar, nice and cosy, and we must go over and join them and make up a party. The Silias family is there too, oh, and did we see little Berta breaking through the crowd? Poor child, she was rather clumsy about it, but she hadn't seemed very well lately anyway. It was a shame about those lovely flowers Berta had been supposed to hand the Führer. 'Beautiful white lilac from Nice! Frau Silias ordered it specially, from the most expensive florist's shop in Frankfurt.' She didn't think much of the way some people threw their money around, but she wouldn't say anything about it on this occasion; on this occasion, only the best was good enough. Personally, however, she'd have chosen roses if it had been her Maria. Roses suited a child better. The Führer would probably prefer roses as well.

You could easily tell that Frau Breitwehr was cross and envious, because she has a daughter of five too, little Maria. When she heard the Führer was coming to Frankfurt she did her best to get little Maria chosen to break through the crowd. But Herr and Frau Silias wanted it to be their little Berta, and

Herr Silias was writing a poem for Berta to say to the Führer.
He worked at it for evenings on end.

All the same, Maria Breitwehr is a prettier child than Berta
and would have been chosen, but Frau Breitwehr had to with-
draw her daughter voluntarily. It was the business of the silver
fox fur rebounding on her. Because Frau Silias knows all about
the trick she played on Herr Breitwehr, and could tell him. *And*
she knows Frau Breitwehr went to a Jewish shop, and she
could let the National Socialist Women's Club know too. Frau
Breitwehr is terrified of all that, so she had to give way and see
Berta Silias chosen as breaker-through-the-crowd.

But Frau Breitwehr still had some hope, because Berta caught
a feverish cold. She had to rehearse her poem for the Führer
all day long, and she got hoarse and complained of a sore throat.
'You ought to put that child to bed, Frau Silias,' Frau Breitwehr
had advised her, only this morning. And Frau Silias had been on
the point of doing just that, but when Frau Breitwehr, of all
people, advised her to do so, she didn't. She wasn't letting Frau
Breitwehr come off best. Moreover, the expensive lilac from
Nice had been paid for, and Herr Silias had written his poem,
and Berta had learnt it, and at last she could say it properly.

We've come to sit at the same tables as the Silias and Breitwehr
party. There are a good many SA and SS men there too. I don't
know all of them. I'm glad we're sitting here. Kurt Pielmann is
talking to friends of his, which takes his mind off Gerti, and Gerti
can't provoke him any more. Herr Kulmbach is sitting beside
me, his face glowing like the rising sun. People are talking and
laughing and screeching. Herr Silias is putting on great airs.
He's fat and pale and greasy, with a few strands of dark hair
over a great, yellow, bald head. His eyes shine like black beetles.
'Another round on me!' he calls. Everyone is merry, everyone's
slightly drunk. Is Herr Silias really going to buy everyone a
drink? How can he manage it? He is asking Gerti what she'd
like, and Kurt Pielmann, and Herr Kulmbach and me. 'It's all on
me today! Where's my little Berta, eh?'

Little Berta is running around the bar, still carrying her bunch
of flowers. The lilac is withering and turning a bit yellow by now,

but you can see it cost a lot. How long does it take a bunch of
flowers to come from Nice to Germany? Surely the flowers
would be tired after a train journey of that length. Maybe they
come by air. We have lilac in Germany too, in May. There are
three big lilac bushes in our garden on the Mosel; they're
beautiful, but the individual flowers aren't as big as the flowers
of this lilac from Nice. I'd love to go to Nice. I'd love to go
abroad some day, I'd . . . 'She just won't let go of those flowers,
will she? Won't let go of them, Berta, eh?' Herr Silias is laughing.
The bouquet is bigger than Berta herself; it's like a bouquet of
flowers running around the bar carrying a child. Berta is wearing
a sky-blue silk dress, already creased and dirty. She is a thin
child, and usually a pale one, but at the moment her cheeks
are red and her eyes bright. Yesterday evening, Frau Silias
dampened her thin, fair hair and plaited it into countless tiny
pigtails, it took her at least three hours. She did everything she
could for the child. At noon today the pigtails were undone, and
Berta has stiff, curly fair hair sticking out from her head.

Frau Silias is sitting there, very quiet and proud. She is a thin,
colourless little woman, and wears cheap nickel-framed glasses
because she's short-sighted.

'Berta!' calls Frau Silias, and then again, 'Berta, do have
something to drink – oh, look what you've done to your dress!
Bed for you in a minute.' Berta is made to drink some hot milk
with a little cognac in it. She has a cold, Frau Silias explains.
The SS men say she did very well all the same. Everyone makes
a fuss of Berta, everyone is talking to her, Herr Kulmbach sits
her on his lap. Herr Silias orders another round of beer and
kirsch, and cigars and cigarettes.

Suddenly, Berta begins crying.

'Hullo, what's the matter?' says Herr Silias. Then he explains
that Berta is upset because the Führer didn't give her his hand.
All present make soothing noises at Berta. Herr Breitwehr buys
her some chocolate, and Berta cheers up again. Kurt Pielmann
tells her she'll have her picture in the paper tomorrow, taken
with the nice SS gentlemen, and she should be proud of herself.

'I know a poem too,' says Berta. Herr Silias beams. He says
Berta must recite the poem. 'You'd like to say it, eh?' He orders

another round. Everyone wants Berta to recite the poem. 'My
husband has a real poetic streak in him,' says Frau Silias, who
doesn't usually say anything much. 'It's high time that child was
in bed,' cries Frau Breitwehr, scowling.

Berta stands on a chair, clutching the bunch of lilac. Her voice
is thin and reedy:

> *'A little German maid you see,*
> *My Führer, and I bring to thee*
> *The fairest flowers of Germany.'*

'Quiet!' a couple of SS men tell their friends around the table,
who are still talking and haven't noticed Berta. 'Keep your
mouths shut. Our little heroine here is saying her poem.'

> *'You gave us back our Army's might . . .'*

'Berta!' Herr Silias is listening attentively, much excited. 'You've
left something out, Berta, didn't you notice?'

Frau Silias straightens Berta's dress, rubbing away at the
dirty marks. 'Drink a little more of your milk, Berta, it's getting
cold.'

'Write that yourself, did you?' Herr Kulmbach asks Herr
Silias. 'You've got a real gift for it! We had someone in my own
family who . . .'

'Quiet, please!'

Berta begins at the beginning again:

> *'A little German maid you see.*
> *A German mother I shall be,*
> *My Führer, and I bring to thee*
> *The fairest flowers of Germany.*
> *You gave us back our Army's might,*
> *Our honour and our will to fight,*
> *And taught us children what is right.'*

'Bravo!' everyone shouts, clapping hard. 'Well done! *Heil* Hitler!
He really ought to have heard that poem, the Führer ought!'

'We'll send it to him,' says Frau Silias, 'but that's not all of it. Do hand me that heavy great bouquet, Berta – oh dear, she *won't* give it up, will she? Such a stubborn child – I don't know where she gets it from.'

> *'No foes we fear: a doughty band*
> *United shall we Germans stand.*
> *A German sun shines on our land*
> *If you, O Führer, on us smile.*
> *Three cheers!*
> Sieg Heil! Sieg Heil! Sieg Heil!'

And Berta goes on shouting, '*Sieg Heil!*' at the top of her voice, on and on, getting redder and redder in the face. '*Sieg Heil!*' Everybody laughs, delighted. Herr Silias is pleased and proud and orders yet another round. Frau Breitwehr can scarcely contain her annoyance, and tells her husband she's had about enough of this and she'd like to go home. Berta is still standing on the chair. She begins reciting the poem all over again.

> *'A little German maid you see.*
> *A German mother I shall be,*
> *My Führer, and I bring to thee*
> *The fairest flowers of . . .'*

But suddenly the big white bunch of lilac is lying on the table. Glasses fall over; the lilac is floating in a puddle of schnapps and beer. Berta is lying on the lilac as if it were a bed, her face buried in the damp and faded flowers. Everyone has jumped up, beer is dripping off the table, some people are mopping their wet suits. 'Now, now, now!' says Herr Silias. 'Bedtime for you!' cries Frau Silias. A waiter comes running up with a dishcloth and turns little Berta over. Her face is a bluish white, her hands are clenched into rigid little fists.

Frau Silias suddenly screams, loud and long.

The proprietor comes over.

The SS men and the rest of us stand there in silence, our feet in the muddy puddles of liquor.

There is a dark forest of people around us, silent, rustling.

A man in a hurry forces his way through the forest of people. 'The waiter called me,' he says. 'I'm a doctor.'

He raises Berta from her lilac bed. He lays her down again, shrugging his shoulders. 'She's gone,' he says, quietly. 'Dead,' he says louder. Frau Silias screams and screams and screams.

'Their bill comes to forty-seven marks,' the proprietor is saying to the waiter, right beside me. 'Who do you suppose we give it to now?'

THREE

I am standing out in the street. My home is the night. Am I drunk? Am I crazy? The voices and sounds all around fall away from me like a coat. I'm freezing. The lights fade out. I am alone.

Little Berta Silias is dead.

We sat together in a corner of the Henninger Bar a little longer: Herr Kulmbach, Gerti, Kurt Pielmann and myself. Gerti was pale and trembling. Kurt Pielmann quietly put a comforting arm around her. Gerti let him, and did not move. Herr Kulmbach was distraught. The whole world suddenly seemed so sad. Only a few of the customers had stayed on. Little Berta had been carried away, and Frau Silias was led out still screaming.

Lights were switched off. The last few customers sat there in a sad, twilight gloom. Their whispered conversation sounded like the pattering of raindrops in the bar.

He himself was not a happy man any more, Herr Kulmbach suddenly confided. He wasn't popular in the Party because he sometimes offered criticism. He used to be one of the seven top SS men in Frankfurt. There's a pub in the Old Town, he said, with a big bone hanging on the wall – the bone of an ox, not a horse. The landlord wouldn't sell horseflesh, he serves nothing but the best, fresh food, you don't have to bother about that so much with horseflesh.

'Like to see that bone, would you?' Kulmbach asked us, his voice sad, full of entreaty. 'We seven Frankfurt SS men carved our names on it. My name's there too. You can see it clear as anything. Hellmuth, that's my first name. I don't have a say in anything now, I don't get promotion, I won't be getting promotion either. Folk get promotion that haven't got half my campaigning experience behind them, but they've got plenty of money, or their parents have plenty of money. And now they can go over my head. It was a different story when we were campaigning. Now you sometimes don't want to go on. What's the point of anything any more? Oh, the tales I could tell you . . .'

They were playing the National Anthem on the radio, so it must be midnight. Herr Kulmbach got to his feet, raising his hand. Other people suddenly stood up here and there in the bar, pale hands raised in the dim light. Next came the Horst Wessel Song, about the brown battalions . . .

'Mind you, 'course the Führer doesn't know the kind of thing that goes on,' said Herr Kulmbach, looking as if he might weep, which would not have surprised me, for he was really rather drunk. He ordered another round of kirsch, and insisted on all of us going on to the pub in the Old Town with the ox-bone on the wall and his name carved on it.

Pielmann and Gerti actually did go off with Kulmbach to look at the bone. The place was open all night, he said, or in any case if he knocked in a certain way they'd always let him in.

I've often noticed how pleased and proud men are at having to knock in a certain way at the doors of perfectly harmless pubs, in order to get in. I expect there are some men who take to politics just for the sake of the secret signals you have to give.

I was rather surprised, at first, to find Gerti was going with them instead of staying with me, but she was very sad, and terribly distraught, and in that sort of state a woman would rather a man she doesn't like for company than a woman she does. A man is a man, after all.

I didn't go with them. I didn't want to be as lonely as I would have been in their company. Pielmann would be comforting Gerti: Gerti always has someone to comfort her, and who have I got? Kulmbach had nothing on his mind but his bone.

And I promised Liska to go and look for Heini, so that's what I'll do.

I wish Franz were here now. He wrote me that letter. 'Dear Sanna . . .'

I am afraid. Fear is rising around me, like rising water, up and up, never stopping. It's like death by drowning. I could go straight home, but what would I do there? I don't feel sleepy. Who loves me? Whom do *I* love?

I'll go and find Heini. At night he always goes to that café in Goethe Street where they serve beer.

There'll soon be wallflowers out in this little square, with flowers like velvet, smelling the same way they look. God help me.

One of dead Berta's little shoes was lying under the table. The proprietor picked it up and fingered it, as if he were planning to keep it as a pledge.

Everything is so sad. I can't help thinking of Franz, and the way his baby brother died. I can't help thinking of Aunt Adelheid, who wanted to see me in prison.

It is nearly three years ago I left Lappesheim and came to Cologne. I arrived at the big railway station. It smelled of dust and hot sunshine. It was a summer afternoon. There was hurry and bustle all around me: sweating people, suitcases in motion. I hadn't come very far, but I was arriving here to start a new life, and I was full of pleasurable apprehension. Suddenly a pair of long black arms went round me, and hard straw scratched my face. It was Aunt Adelheid, scratching my face with her hard straw hat instead of kissing me with her mouth. I felt at once we weren't going to love each other, and I hadn't even seen her face yet. Then I did see it. It was sharp and grey, with narrow, dark, glittering eyes. Aunt Adelheid's voice was shrill and sharp. Everything about her pierced and cut you. I felt like crying.

Then somebody took my hand. And didn't say anything, just looked at me quietly and thoroughly. He was tall and thin, with a pair of patient shoulders. He had a pale, serious face, and I thought his brow looked gentle and thoughtful, though it didn't seem particularly striking. His eyes and brow and mouth and shoulders, in fact, all looked a blur to me, smudged and running together. All I could really see clearly was the glaringly bright red silk scarf he was wearing. It looked ridiculous. What man wears a scarf like that? Then I saw the man's arms. They hung by his sides, long and sad, like the arms of captive apes with no real reason left for climbing, so that their long arms now seem superfluous.

The man was Aunt Adelheid's son Franz, my cousin.

I thought he was crazy. I felt like laughing.

I didn't laugh; I didn't cry.

Franz carried my case for me. His long arm got even longer, his patient shoulders more patient than ever.

Franz works in a solicitor's office, but he'll never get to be head clerk. He has his strengths, but they're not the sort that get you anywhere in normal life. He has no friends, because his nature is a sad and lonely one. He has no ambition: he doesn't want to do better than other people. He seldom says anything much, so what are people supposed to make of him? And he always concentrates on one thing at a time, which tends to make other people nervous. If he picks a glass up, then he will be concentrating entirely on the holding of that glass, unable to think or feel anything else. When he looks at a stone, he's entirely caught up in the sight of that stone, and can't talk or listen at the same time. When he eats, he eats. And when he loves, he loves.

Sometimes he seems to be living wrapped in thick veils. When you speak to him, he wakes up without actually having been asleep. Nobody knows what he is thinking or dreaming of inside those veils. He may know himself, but he doesn't talk about it. He just lives, and that's all there is to say. When you merge into life you can't describe the feeling.

But perhaps he sometimes thinks how he killed a baby. The baby was his little brother.

There is a photograph of this baby hanging over the sofa where Aunt Adelheid sits at mealtimes. The upholstery of the sofa is threadbare. It was once green, and then went yellow with time and the sunlight that filters into the room grudgingly, but constantly.

The place always smells of rancid fat and rank cabbage, because there is no door between it and the kitchen, which consists of nothing but a small gas stove and a sink. The kitchen lies on one side of the room and the stationery shop on the other. There are some crackers lying on a small table next to the counter. I could always see those crackers from my chair at the dining table. They looked creased and purple, like withered lilac. Old as the hills they were, made of weary, crumpled crêpe paper. You weren't allowed to clear them away, because Aunt Adelheid thought perhaps she'd sell them yet. And then perhaps she hoped she wouldn't. A blond commercial traveller from Cologne had left her this consignment of crackers years ago. She once told me about him. Naturally it's a sad thing for a woman when a man sleeps with her and then makes off, leaving nothing behind but crackers. And when instead of a love letter, all she gets is an invoice for the crackers from the man's firm.

The dead baby's photograph hangs over the sofa, opposite Franz's place at the table. Its frame is made of silver, twisted so that it's supposed to look like a wreath of flowers. The picture itself shows Aunt Adelheid sitting holding a baby with a bald head and a long lacy dress. The infant in baby's evening dress was burnt to death.

Franz was three years old at the time, a resident of Lappesheim, though you can't say such a little boy is actually residing anywhere, he just exists. Aunt Adelheid's ramshackle little house stood in Ufer Street, jammed in between two larger houses which almost crushed it. Its roof was made of slate the silvery-grey colour of a raven in flight. The roof was defective and the windows cracked, for Aunt Adelheid's husband was not a builder or a glazier but a tailor, and if people along the Mosel can't do a thing for themselves they don't employ other folk to do it for them.

He was a good tailor, and always very cheerful. First Aunt Adelheid did for his cheerfulness, and then he died of TB. He left two children, Franz, aged three, and little Sebastian, aged six months.

Aunt Adelheid was down by the ferry, talking to the woman there, moaning about her late husband's death. She never had a good word to say for him when he was alive, wouldn't let him go to the pub, wouldn't so much as let him smile. But once he was good and dead she wept and wailed over him. Suddenly the ferry woman saw people running about in Ufer Street in agitation, shouting and waving. There was smoke coming out of Aunt Adelheid's house, pouring out of the windows. And there was a bright and flickering glow in the street. The crowd bunched closer together. 'Fire!' shouted several young fellows, hoarse and loud and long, to give the volunteer fire brigade the alarm. Aunt Adelheid staggered towards her house. She was weak at the knees, she collapsed and then stood up again. Segebrecht, the pub landlord, came towards her, limping in a stiff, slow way, black as the Devil with soot. People stood back to form a rigid, silent alleyway. Aunt Adelheid and Herr Segebrecht were approaching each other from opposite ends of this alley. Segebrecht was carrying something black and crumpled. There was a little rag of singed, blue wool dangling from the black thing – Aunt Adelheid tottered, and all the women suddenly screamed in chorus.

Little Franz had lit the fire. He was proud of knowing how to do it. People had rescued him from a blazing room, and while Segebrecht carried poor dead little Sebastian towards Aunt Adelheid, Franz stood there outside the burning house, hands clasped in front of the fire, eyes shining with happiness.

Nobody loved Franz any more. Not the people in the village, not his mother. In her desperation, she just wouldn't believe that if it was anyone's fault it was hers. Why had she left two tiny children on their own? She wanted someone to take the blame, so it had to be little Franz. As time went by Aunt Adelheid idolized dead little Sebastian more and more, constantly weeping and praying by his grave.

If Franz was going to be loved too, even a tiny little bit, he'd have had to die as well. He went very quiet, and stayed that way. He didn't learn to talk early, or have any fun learning, because nobody wanted to speak to him. People avoided him, and he had to get used to being silent and lonely.

I didn't like Franz myself at first. And then I came to like him because Aunt Adelheid didn't. I wanted to be nice to him; it was so sad and horrible to see the way Aunt Adelheid tormented him. Franz had to put flowers and leaves round the photograph of little Sebastian before dinner every Sunday. Aunt Adelheid gave him the flowers and leaves to be arranged separately, and then sat on a chair in silence watching Franz's hands, which sometimes shook and let the flowers drop. And then Aunt Adelheid would look at him sternly, without a word, and Franz went red and bent down to pick the flowers up. 'I am surprised, but glad, that you can bring yourself to eat,' she sometimes said in a slow, chanting sort of voice, at which Franz would put down his knife and fork, with hopeless despair in his eyes, his arms hanging long and thin by his sides.

One day I couldn't stand it any more. I shouted at Aunt Adelheid. She was so surprised she couldn't answer back. I don't remember exactly what I said, except that the drift of it was the accident was her own fault, hers and *not* Franz's, he'd only been a tiny child at the time without any idea what he was doing. And it was her fault little Sebastian was killed, and her fault Franz was unhappy. And if little Sebastian was an angel in heaven now, he'd be very sad about his mother and he would love Franz very much. Aunt Adelheid never forgave me for saying all this, but there was a happy look in Franz's eyes.

I did want to be nice to him, but then I made some friends and went out dancing with them in the evening now and then, and I felt embarrassed when Franz came to see me home, with his silent face and his patient ape-like arms and his ridiculous red scarf. We'd be sitting in the middle of a lot of noise, and he was tranquil. He would sit there at our table, grave and friendly. He did nothing to trouble us, and yet it *was* troubling. So the others laughed louder and louder in their annoyance, as if to smother him with their laughter. They made jokes about him which didn't bother him a bit, because he didn't understand the jokes. Then they laughed even more angrily. Once they tried making him drunk, but he didn't get drunk.

There were some very smart and self-assured girls among my friends, and I went to no end of trouble to try and be like them. The boys put on airs as well; I was afraid they'd think me silly and stupid. Often I joined in their laughter, afraid they might notice I didn't really understand what they were laughing at. I wanted them to admire me as much as they admired themselves. It was fear made me want to be one of them; they were always ganging up on someone, one person at a time, and I didn't want them ganging up on me. So I went along with them over Franz, making even nastier jokes about him than they did. I felt proud when they laughed at my jokes, but I was ashamed of myself too.

When I had to pay a quick visit to the Ladies and got out of the noise and the laughter, I used to feel sad and disgusted. I'd leave the Ladies as fast as I could, scared even to take the time to comb my hair. I was afraid the others would be laughing at me while I was gone, as indeed they were.

Franz went on being nice, and I went on being nasty.

One day there was an exhibition in Cologne, in the Neumarkt: an exhibition of venereal diseases and the consequences of inter-racial breeding within a nation. It was organized by the Strength Through Joy movement. Aunt Adelheid and I went to see it, because there was nothing indecent about it, it was in the cause of scientific explanation, so it was our duty to go.

I was fairly well used to the idea of horrors, from what they had told us at gas mask drill, but now I was actually *seeing* eroded embryos preserved in spirit. And pictures of little babies whose eyes were just hollows full of yellowish-green pus. Women whose deformed breasts and buttocks touched the ground. Models of old men looking like crazy little children, and little children looking like ancient, wrinkled old men. And blood and pus and sticky red sores everywhere. All as a result of venereal diseases and inter-racial breeding. And then people have to go inventing poison gas too. Makes you quite surprised, speaking as a human being, to be alive at all and not have your entire body eaten away.

We were studying the eroded noses section when an elderly gentleman came up and spoke to Aunt Adelheid. He took his hat off, very politely. 'I believe we've met, ma'am,' he said. His head was bald and round and brownish-grey, and his lower lip was thick and red, drooping like a mattress hung out of the window to air.

'Why, so we have, Assistant Secretary!' said Aunt Adelheid, beaming in a proud and happy way.

We got into conversation. The Assistant Secretary – his post was in the Civil Service – always used to buy his notebooks at

Aunt Adelheid's shop. 'A shocking sight, eh?' he said, pointing to the eroded noses.

'Yes, indeed,' said Aunt Adelheid gravely. 'Terrible, everyone ought to see it, it's a warning to us all.' Don't ask me why Aunt Adelheid needed a warning. She was over fifty, with no chance left of catching a venereal disease. Unless she got it from eating unwashed fruit off a barrow in the street.

The Assistant Secretary saw us home. He was very earnest and very polite.

He took to calling at the shop to buy notebooks quite often. His name is Ludwig Wittkamp; Aunt Adelheid told me so. It's quite surprising to find an important official like an Assistant Secretary has an ordinary personal name of his own. What does he need one for? He lives in the Hohenzollernring, though it is also hard to imagine him going about the ordinary business of living.

He bought the cheapest little notebooks he could find in our shop. He thinks highly of orderliness, and writes down all his expenses. Especially when he goes away, because that's when your expenses can get right out of hand, before you know it you've spent a whole three marks and can't say where it went.

One day the Assistant Secretary invited me out to the 'Beery Donkey' to eat mussels. I felt very proud, and wrote home, and to my friend Josefine Leyendecker in Lappesheim, telling them how I was mixing frequently with Assistant Secretaries and suchlike important persons. Mussels are cheap. I've always liked them. The Assistant Secretary didn't have any mussels for fear of food poisoning. He said he never ate mushrooms either. Or raw meat.

The restaurant was full of the smell of food, and restless people eating greedily and talking. The Assistant Secretary had knuckle of veal and salad. Salads are healthy, full of vitamins.

My mussels looked like squashed embryos. They reminded me of the exhibition of venereal diseases where I'd met the Assistant Secretary. I felt sick. I could have done with a Boone-kamp to drink, but I didn't like to ask for one.

The Assistant Secretary was cross because I left nearly all my mussels, but they still had to be paid for. He told me he

could get through a whole bottle of wine in an evening, within
four or five hours. Back home in Lappesheim, we'd get through
four bottles in that time.

He invited me to go home and share a bottle of wine with him
afterwards. At the moment he was drinking gin, as a stimulant
and because the knuckle of veal had been fatty. Then he talked
to me like an important official and an educated man, i.e.
seriously and politically and erotically. He said that as a Catholic
he had to fight against his sexual desires, which were something
tremendous. He felt drawn to prostitutes, down into those wild
depths of life where you lose your money and your health and
your soul's salvation. That was why he fought the good fight
against his desires. He admired the Führer, and supported him
fervently as the saviour of the German nation when it was in
danger of humiliation at the hands of enemy foreigners. But
being a Catholic he was against Rosenberg, who had written
some kind of mystical or mythological book about the twentieth
century and the Germanic peoples. All this was very hard to
understand.

Then the Assistant Secretary said he yearned for marriage,
since only in Christian marriage could he give free rein to his
desires. It was all right then. I thought I'd love to be an Assistant
Secretary's wife, on account of Aunt Adelheid and everyone in
Lappesheim. But then I'd have to put up with the free rein of
those alarming desires. I couldn't picture that part of it.

Anyway, I didn't have to wrestle with the problem of whether
to marry him or not, because *he* didn't want to marry *me*. The
only wife who would do for him was one with a dowry, and
property, and who was young and pretty and willing to work
into the bargain. Well, where would I get a dowry and property?

The Assistant Secretary had thought I'd be inheriting the
thriving pub in Lappesheim, and getting money from my humble
but well-to-do father before that, in which case he wouldn't
have objected to my common origins. Because he himself is
wonderfully well educated. He told me how he stood by the
grave of someone called Hölderlin and read a poem by this
Hölderlin. Not just once, either; several times. These were
always edifying moments. All this was so sacred to him that he

couldn't talk about it, couldn't even mention it. He went on to talk about it.

I said I didn't have any property, but I wasn't poor. Then he fell silent for a while, drummed his fingers crossly on the table, had another gin, and then said well, he'd like to share a bottle of wine at home with me all the same. He said I looked like a skinny little schoolgirl.

All of a sudden there was Franz, standing by our table. His face was pale, his eyes calm, his scarf resplendent. Oh, if only I hadn't told him I'd be here with the Assistant Secretary this evening! The idiot – coming to take me home when I was out with a posh, worldly-wise Assistant Secretary!

'Good evening,' said Franz. I wasn't going to give him my hand. 'Would you like to come home now, Sanna? It's raining – I brought you a coat.' That stupid voice, so soft and velvety. What can you do about a pale-blue sort of voice like that? You can't argue with it, you can't get angry with it, you can't laugh at it. What does someone like Franz want with a voice anyway? He himself seems quite surprised to have one.

'Do sit down, won't you?' said the Assistant Secretary, very correct and decidedly annoyed. Franz sat down slowly, back very straight. He laid his long thin hands carefully on the table, as if about to pray.

The Assistant Secretary drew the corners of his mouth down scornfully and said well, it was nice for me to have such a gallant cousin to squire me about, and did I still feel like that bottle of wine? There was no need for the young gentleman to worry: he, the Assistant Secretary, would take me home by car.

'Yes,' said Franz, and stayed put instead of going away.

'For goodness' sake, do take that ridiculous scarf off!' I said. My voice sounded shrill in my own ears. When he did take the scarf off, I felt as if I'd torn it from his neck with my own hands. The Assistant Secretary laughed. Franz looked sadly stripped and naked without it. The scarf lay on the pale wooden bench beside him, red and warm.

Franz was given his scarf by Paul. Paul is Franz's one friend. He is a fat, cheerful, red ball of a man. Franz found him in the Municipal Woods quite late one evening, when the place was deserted. Paul was lying in the middle of the road; a motorcyclist had run over him and didn't stop. He wasn't dead, but he *had* been run over, and he was still drunk too. The next car that came along would have finished him off. Franz dragged Paul off the road and helped him get home. That sort of thing, naturally, can lead to friendship. The two of them don't have much to say to one another, but you can sense the friendly affection between them.

Paul sometimes comes to the shop and annoys Aunt Adelheid by eating and drinking anything he can find in the kitchen, and taking postcards from the stand without paying for them. He gave Franz his scarf. Perhaps someone had given it to *him* and he felt ashamed to wear something so daft. No, that's not right. Paul meant to give Franz the scarf as a handkerchief – it's really a big silk square. But Franz thought it was too good for that, so he wore it round his neck, out of friendship and because he was pleased to have it.

The waiter brought Franz a glass of beer. No one had ordered it, but Franz didn't send it back.

The Assistant Secretary said well, now he saw I was in good company, he might as well go. I still don't understand why, but at the time I was terrified the Assistant Secretary's feelings had been hurt, and I wanted to go with him.

Suddenly a draught of air moved the red silk scarf on the bench. It looked as if it were breathing. The dark felt curtains at the door of the restaurant were pushed back a little way and a girl slipped through them. She was small and fair and delicate, like a Christmas fairy, all white and gold. But she was soaked with rain. She stopped beside our table, which was right by the entrance. You could hear the rain pelting down in the street outside. A waiter showed the girl one of the few empty seats in the restaurant, but she didn't want to sit down; she shook her head, embarrassed and shy. I'd been just as shy myself, a few months back. Now I felt very fine and superior, compared to her. *And* she probably didn't have any money. Her blouse was cheap and shoddy. I'd have wanted paying to wear a thing like that. She looked prettier than I ever did. I was glad the waiter showed his contempt by pointedly taking no notice of her.

She'd only been standing there beside us for a moment before she turned to escape back out into the rain, having just escaped from it into the restaurant. Then Franz looked at her. She looked at Franz. My heart was thudding; there was a rushing in my ears, like red-hot wheels. The Assistant Secretary said something, but his voice was far away and I couldn't hear him. Franz was giving this rain-soaked girl all in white and gold my coat. What did he think the idea was? *My* coat! It had been lying on his lap all this time, it was mine, he'd brought it for *me*. 'Here,' he told the rain-soaked girl, 'put this on and I'll see you home.' What business had he speaking to a strange girl in his soft, velvety voice? What business had she looking at him with such a gentle, dark-blue light in her eyes? This was too much! 'Sanna,' said Franz, 'Sanna, you're going by car, you won't need a coat. I'll bring it back to you later.'

'I'm not going in any car, Franz – I do need my coat – let me have it! Now! Is the bill settled, waiter? Good night, Assistant Secretary. Come on, Franz, please,' I said. 'I don't want to go home in the rain on my own. I've got your scarf in my bag.'

I didn't sleep downstairs at Aunt Adelheid's, on the same floor as herself and Franz. There wouldn't have been room for me. I slept in the same building, but up in an attic which also belonged to Aunt Adelheid, next to old Herr Pütz's apartment. My attic room was small and bare: damp and cold in winter and very hot in summer. Franz had never been up there with me.

'Please come up, Franz,' I said. 'I'm scared to be alone tonight. I'm scared I won't be able to sleep.'

Dark, cold, sticky, misty air crept in through the cracks around my window. My hands were stiff with cold, my face was burning. It had stopped raining outside; the sky was quiet. And the room was full of deafening silence. Franz stood by the door, tall, upright, silent, his face turned to the wall. Far away, a car hooted its horn.

The small electric bulb hanging from the ceiling cast a dim, dirty orange light. My bed looked like a piece of orange peel. I took off my shoes and stockings. 'That Assistant Secretary is a disgusting old man, Franz. I'm never going out with him again.'

I took my dress off. 'Here's the chair, Franz – sit down. I hope your mother won't realize you're up here with me. Goodness knows what she'd think. Why do people have to think goodness knows what about something perfectly harmless? I think it's horrible of them. I don't understand it.'

I took my vest off. 'Don't turn round for a moment, Franz.' Why didn't he move, why didn't he say something? 'I don't think I could bear it here in Cologne without you, Franz.' I was lying in bed in my cheap, ugly, white nightie. Will I ever have a silk nightie? 'You can turn round now, Franz, it's all right. Supposing I was ill, you'd come and visit me and see me looking just like this.'

But I wasn't ill.

Franz was still standing there, silent, not moving, his throat all pale and white; it looked thin and naked and helpless without the bright red scarf I made him take off. This was the first time I'd ever seen him without his red scarf. I felt ashamed. I wanted to go on and on feeling ashamed. 'Good night, Franz, I'm tired. Give me your hand.'

He gave me his hand.

And when the soft, gentle light of dawn slowly came in to brighten my room, I got up quietly and opened the window. The air seemed to be singing, hovering, and my heart was light and calm and happy as the earth after a thunderstorm. I took the bright red silk scarf out of my black handbag. It was a bit crumpled, and I tried to smooth it out.

Franz lay in my bed, sleeping deep and soundly. I had to laugh, because even his snoring sounded soft and velvety. I put the red silk scarf in his dear sleeping hands.

FOUR

Although Aunt Adelheid didn't care a bit about Franz, she still wanted him to belong to her body and soul, not to anybody else at all. It annoyed her no end to see Franz getting more cheerful, while she had hardly any power to torment him now. Seeing Aunt Adelheid insisted on having fresh flowers round that dead baby's photograph every Sunday, I simply took to arranging them on Sundays myself, without stopping to ask her. For Franz, it was like being released from a curse, and Aunt Adelheid lost interest in the wreathing of the picture. At last there came a Sunday when it got no wreath at all, because she had forgotten to buy the fresh flowers.

Of course she soon ferreted out the fact that there was something going on between Franz and me. Well, we didn't go to much trouble to hide it. Franz told her we were planning to get married in one or two years' time, and how could she actually object? Hitherto Franz had been giving his mother his entire salary, getting just a little bit of pocket money now and then. Now he gave her only half of it, and saved up the rest of the money for our future. We were thinking of opening a shop some day. I thought a tobacconist's would be best. We wouldn't have needed much initial capital, because the cigarette firms give you credit, and you could begin in an area where shop rents are really cheap. Later on, we might sell newspapers and magazines and stationery too, and we could add a little lending library as well. Franz and I often liked to lay such plans. We enjoyed it.

Aunt Adelheid tried to annoy us and spite us in any way she could, but we didn't much mind: there were two of us, after all, and we were of the same mind. When there are two of you, you can laugh at a good many things which would make you cry on your own.

All the same, Aunt Adelheid managed to ruin practically everything for us with the help of politics. It was like this:

We'd gone out for a walk one Saturday, in the middle of the day, Franz and myself and Franz's friend Paul. Paul is short and round and fat, not a man you'd fall in love with, but I was extremely fond of him. As soon as he came rolling up you felt like laughing. He worked in a hardware factory in the Ehrenfeld district.

That Saturday, he'd invited Franz and me out for a glass of local Cologne beer in the Päffgen Bar. We were very cheerful, and we had a gin as well. Then, unfortunately, I had to go back to serve in the shop, because Aunt Adelheid was having a coffee party that afternoon. Franz and Paul came too, to keep me company, and in return I promised to pinch them something to eat from the kitchen on the sly.

Aunt Adelheid was sitting in the shop with Fräulein Fricke, an old maid who keeps house for her brother. We were in good time; the rest of the women coming to the hen-party wouldn't arrive for another half hour or more.

Fräulein Fricke was deep in political conversation with Aunt Adelheid. 'Before the first of March, you know, I used to cry – every night, I used to cry, and if I didn't cry I prayed, and what did I look like?'

'Oh, dear me, you looked terrible.'

'But I don't cry nowadays, do I, and I don't need to pray any more, and I'm looking better too now, aren't I?'

'Oh, dear me, yes, you're looking better too now.'

'Trust, you see, that's all we need, and the Führer will do the rest.'

They went on talking about the Führer, and Fräulein Fricke said she'd made a little altar to him in her room, with candles burning all the time.

I could tell Paul wanted to provoke Aunt Adelheid and Fräulein Fricke, who is always a bit peculiar. That was fine by me. Paul produced a newspaper showing the main differences between National Socialists and criminals. On the left, there were pictures of the heads of Gauleiters, group leaders and other high-up Nazis, and on the right there were the heads of pickpockets, rapists, robbers, murderers and suchlike. Paul hid the captions below the pictures and got the two women to guess who was a National Socialist and who was a criminal. They actually guessed wrong three times running, which amused Paul a lot and made both ladies furious. Paul said it didn't say much for their sound German instincts if they could take a National Socialist for a criminal, and vice versa.

The atmosphere in the little shop was so thick you could have cut it with a knife. There was a hot and angry gleam in Aunt Adelheid's eyes, and Fräulein Fricke's breath was coming all thin and whistling. I switched the radio on in the next room. There was a concert on gramophone records. Then they said Göring would be talking on the radio that evening. All the ladies were going to stay at Aunt Adelheid's to hear him. Thinking nothing of it, I said I'd rather *not* hear him, because I always got the feeling he was telling me off. And that was absolutely all I said on the subject, but even so it was far too much. It's true, though: one of those speeches begins harmlessly enough, going on about the magnificent German nation which will overcome everything, and you feel you're being praised and flattered for listening to it. Then the radio lets out a sudden flood of abuse, saying everyone who offends against the nation's will for reconstruction will be smashed, and those who go in for harmful, carping criticism will be destroyed.

My heart always stands still when I hear those speeches, because how do I know I'm not one of the sort who are going to be smashed? And the worst of it is that I just don't understand what's really going on. I'm only gradually getting the hang of the things you must be careful not to do.

And back at Aunt Adelheid's at that time, I was a good deal dimmer than I am today. But even then I was scared stiff someone might notice I didn't understand a word of it. Göring and the other ministers often shout over the radio, very loud and clear and angry. 'There are still some who have not understood what it is all about, but we shall know how to deal with them.' I hate hearing that kind of thing, it's creepy, because I still don't know what it *is* all about, or what they mean. And it's far too dangerous to ask anyone. Judging by things I've picked up from what I've heard and read, I could be either criminal or of chronically unsound mind. Neither of which must come out or I'll be done for. If I'm criminal I'll go to prison, and if I'm of chronically unsound mind they'll operate on me so that I can't get married and have children.

The long and the short of it is that I still don't know any more today, but I'm cleverer than I was then, when I told Aunt Adelheid and Fräulein Fricke I didn't want to listen to speeches on the radio.

We went on to talk about all our speechifying Party men, in a perfectly harmless way, and Fräulein Fricke and Aunt Adelheid started going on about the Führer again. They thought he was absolutely marvellous. Aunt Adelheid told us about the wild enthusiasm that filled her when she heard the Führer speak in the Exhibition Hall in Cologne. Paul asked her what she had particularly liked about it, and I said, 'She liked the way he was sweating.' Fräulein Fricke immediately clasped her hands in horror above her head, as if I'd said the most dreadful thing in the world. And I couldn't explain, because a woman came into the shop just then to buy postcards with pictures of dogs on them. Aunt Adelheid disappeared into the room behind the shop with Fräulein Fricke, and I felt perfectly happy again, idiot that I was, and hadn't the faintest notion that the two ladies were planning to twist my words into a rope to hang me with.

It's a fact that the way the Führer was sweating *did* make a bigger impression on Aunt Adelheid than anything else. She said so herself, too. I was in the hall with her while the Führer was speaking. He shouted like mad and was in a state of tremendous excitement. I couldn't make out a word of it. So I asked Aunt Adelheid what he had been saying afterwards, and asked her to explain the speech to me. It turned out that Aunt Adelheid couldn't tell me a single thing the Führer had said, but she did say, quivering with enthusiasm, 'Wasn't it wonderful? Have you ever known anything like it? Did you notice how he could hardly speak at all, and went white as a sheet and nearly collapsed? That man spares himself nothing. Did you see the way he was bathed in sweat at the end of the speech, and then the SS surrounded him?' Well, that was what Aunt Adelheid said, and

I saw it myself. Aunt Adelheid feels just the same in the City Theatre. I've been there with her a couple of times. She doesn't think anything much of the actors in comedies. But we saw a play called *Thomas Paine*, where there was an actor down in a dungeon, wearing clanking chains and ranting away so that you were fairly deafened. 'It goes right through you,' said Aunt Adelheid. And when the actor took his bow she said, 'Look, he's utterly exhausted, bathed in sweat, what a wonderful actor, we ought to see this play more often.' And then she even bought a photograph of the actor and hung it in her bedroom. The Führer's hanging there too.

So I had every right to assume that the most important point, to Aunt Adelheid, is for someone to sweat.

Three days after that Saturday, there was a brisk, firm knock at my attic door at seven in the morning. At first I thought it was Aunt Adelheid on a spying trip to see if Franz was sleeping with me, but he'd gone an hour ago. I tried to go back to sleep instead of answering the door. Then there was more knocking – thump, thump, thump – and loud, harsh men's voices.

A couple of minutes later two deadly serious men were crawling about under my bed, looking under the mattress, into my suitcase, even looking in the chamber pot. 'Secret police,' they had said abruptly when I opened the door, and after that they wouldn't answer any of my questions.

The men went on creating chaos down in Aunt Adelheid's apartment. 'Oh, the shame of it!' cried Aunt Adelheid. 'And in my home – the shame of it! I'm a respectable widow, I've been in the movement for years . . .'

'Yes, yes, we know,' one of the men told Aunt Adelheid gently, all kindness. 'It's nothing to do with you.'

'If I'd known what I was taking into my home!' cried Aunt Adelheid, looking at me as if I'd taken part in some dreadful jewel robbery.

The whole thing seemed to me utterly unreal; I thought maybe I was still dreaming. I hadn't even been allowed to get dressed to go downstairs with the men, they just let me fling my raincoat on. And the silly thing was that Franz wasn't there, because he went out to buy vegetables at the market before

office hours. Then the two men let Aunt Adelheid go upstairs
to fetch me some clothes, while they stood guard over me.
They'd searched and searched and found nothing, and they were
looking even grimmer than before.

Then they took me to police headquarters in a car, and I had
to sit in the Gestapo room upstairs for hours on end.

I didn't know what I was supposed to be there for. People
kept coming in and making statements. Natives of Cologne had
tales to tell of other natives of Cologne who had dealings with
the Red Front. An old, old woman came in and went on for
hours about her lodger, who didn't pay his rent and was a
Communist. She said he'd torn down the swastika flag she
draped over the balcony. Well, no, she didn't actually see him
do it, but the swastika flag had been torn down all right, and
she'd given the man her best front room, with her late husband's
armchair and all, her late husband had been a policeman – 'I
brought a picture to show you, Commissioner, look, that's him'
– yes, well, she'd put his armchair in that room. And the lodger
hadn't paid any rent for three months '. . . and the swastika flag
on the balcony was ever so nice, Commissioner, oh, you should
just have seen it – my brother's a witness too, he's out there in
the waiting room . . .' And in comes the brother with a friend,
both of them even more ancient than the old lady, shrivelled old
men with their hats in their hands, and humble eyes. The
policeman's old widow begins crying over the swastika flag and
the unpaid rent. 'She's a bit soft in the head, see?' says the
brother. 'And what with all the excitement, and the strain on an
old woman – she's got water on the legs, see? Hasn't gone out
in the street for years.' Then he says he's due to inherit, and
after his sister's death he'll have a right to the rent which the
Communist isn't paying now, and the man won't move out of his
room either. How do they know he's a Communist? Well,
everything about him shows it. The old folk go on about it for
hours, and the officer takes all they say down on his typewriter.
There are three typewriters in the room, clattering away steadily
and inexorably. And people keep coming in the whole time to
inform on someone or other. You'd think the whole of Cologne
had made a date to meet in this shabby, grey Gestapo room.

An old man comes in with a fourteen-year-old boy. 'Chief Commissioner, sir, it's about my son. Father of my grandson here. Frau Fabrizius on the first floor – we live in Weyer Street, see? – well, Frau Fabrizius informed against him, said he fell downstairs drunk and said something rude about Herr Göring. Herr Göring the Minister. Well, Chief Commissioner, sir, here's my grandson can swear to it, see? – come here, Pitter – now then, Pitter, when your father came home, did you open the door, eh? And heard him stumble a bit and let out a curse or so and that's all, right? Can you swear to it, eh?' The lad nods. 'See, it's only because Frau Fabrizius is always quarrelling with my daughter-in-law, it started in the laundry room, see, and then . . .

'Where is my husband?' There's a woman standing among the typewriters all of a sudden, her face pale and her hair straggling. She is very pregnant. I jump up, all the people who have had complaints laid against them and are seated at intervals along the walls jump up, so that she can sit down. You can see she might go into labour any minute. 'Where is my husband? He was taken away all of a sudden at nine last night, he'd got the dole book and the dole money in his pocket, I haven't any money and I'm about to have my baby, where is my husband?' The typewriters clatter and clatter away. 'Give us your address, my good woman,' says the officer, 'it will be all right, just calm down.' But the woman is perfectly calm and firm. 'Where is my husband?'

And more and more people keep coming in. This Gestapo room seems to be a positive place of pilgrimage. Mothers are informing on their daughters-in-law, daughters on their fathers-in-law, brothers on their sisters, sisters on their brothers, friends on their friends, drinking companions on their drinking companions, neighbours on their neighbours. And the typewriters go clatter, clatter, clatter, all the statements are taken down, all the informers are treated well and kindly. Now and then mothers whose sons have disappeared turn up, wives whose husbands have disappeared, sisters whose brothers have disappeared, children whose parents have disappeared, friends whose friends have disappeared. People making these inquiries are not so well and kindly treated as the informers . . . by the time my turn to be questioned came, after hours and hours, there was nothing in my head but confused thoughts and nothing in my ears but that constant clattering and questioning and talking and roaring of noise. I was so tired I hardly minded what happened. I was not afraid, not even curious as to what would become of me.

I had to give my name, age, place of birth and religion. Just the same as everyone else. Had I ever been an active Communist, what were my political views, what sort of people did I mix with, had I ever been a member of any political or religious association, what were my feelings about National Socialism – I was never asked so many questions in all my life! And then it began in earnest: I was said to have made subversive statements about Göring's speeches on the radio, and disparaging remarks running down the Führer. I was not a bit surprised, because I had long since realized it was Aunt Adelheid who had landed me in this mess. I tried to explain it all, but the officer looked so stern and chilly that I thought explanation might only make matters worse. So I had to sign a statement saying I had said I didn't want to listen to Göring telling me off over the radio. And the best thing about the Führer's speech was the way he had been sweating.

After I'd signed this statement I was taken down to the magistrate who had powers of summary jurisdiction. He talked to me like a priest at a cut-price funeral. He was still a young man, and very full of his own importance.

'Now,' he said, 'this question is strictly between ourselves – what did you vote at the last election?' I said I was only eighteen and not old enough to vote yet. He spent half an hour telling me he could take me into protective custody here and now, and what did I think of that? What on earth was I supposed to think of that? He had a sort of gleam in his eyes – if he'd tried to kiss me I'd have kicked him in the belly as hard as I could, he could have perished before my eyes for all I cared, the brute. But if he was going to take me into protective custody I'd have to put up with it.

The voice of this powerful little young man clacked on and

on, the room was small and grey and like a prison – a handful of dim sunlight shone in on dust and grey files. I was desperate with weariness. Was I going to have to stay here all my life? Suddenly I remembered something Paul had said. I'll never forget the evening when he told us about countries where you can say what you like, where you don't have anything to fear as long as you don't break God's ten commandments. There are countries, he said, without any hidden dangers, where you can greet people any way you like – and you can weep on days of rejoicing and laugh on days of mourning, just depending how you feel at the time.

And suddenly it was all too much for me. Here I sat, going to be punished and I didn't know why. I didn't know what was good any more, I didn't know what was bad any more. I thought of those countries obeying God's ten commandments, where good is good and bad is bad. I thought of the far-off foreign lands Paul talked about. I could not keep from crying harder than I'd ever cried in all my life before.

The young magistrate thought I must be crying for remorse or fear. He was pleased to see me crying in front of him, and he let me go.

Down by the big doorway I collided with a very old woman hauling a big, shabby suitcase along.

'Don't cry,' the old lady told me, 'don't you cry now, I'll make sure he gets something to eat – here, look at this!' And she tapped the big case she had put down beside her in a mysterious way. A young policeman came along. His face was pale. You don't really see anything of a policeman but his helmet, never his face. 'She's off her head,' he told me, pointing at the little old lady smiling away to herself. 'Her son's been in a concentration camp for seven months – used to be a mate of ours here. Nobody knows if he's still alive. His mother went off her head, won't eat, spends all day making sandwiches, it's always sandwiches, and packs them in that case and brings them here. She's afraid he isn't getting enough to eat. Won't rest until she's got the case upstairs to the Gestapo office. They always send her and her case away again, and she always comes back. There's no helping her, or not much anyway.' The young policeman picked the case up. 'Come on, Granny dear, I'll carry your case upstairs,' he said. The tiny little old woman beamed. 'Oh, that's good of you, sir, that really is. Now don't cry, miss, he'll get something to eat now.'

I rushed home. I must get away, I kept thinking, I must get away from here.

Outside the shop I met Franz. I dragged him upstairs to the attic with me. 'I must pack a case. I must get away.'

Franz still had no idea of what had happened to me. I told him while I collected my things – it may have sounded a bit muddled, a bit hasty and confused. 'But where are you going, then?' was all Franz asked, lips white and trembling, instead of rushing downstairs in a rage and slamming his mother into the wall so hard she'd stick there. 'Stay here,' he said, 'stay here, nothing else will happen, I'll talk to Mother.' 'You get out of here!' I shouted at him. What's the point of talking to an idiot who doesn't understand?

'Yes, but where are you going?' was all Franz kept asking. Where? Well, maybe to Lappesheim, or – and at this moment it occurred to me I might go to Algin in Frankfurt. He'd invited me several times. Anyway, I was practically beside myself, what with Franz failing to understand I'd be safer anywhere in the world than in his mother's house. And I was in mortal danger living with a woman who hated me because she had to pay me money from the shop – and hated me because it was on my account Franz gave her only half his salary. That alone would have been reason enough for her to get me into a concentration camp, just to be rid of me. I suddenly saw it all, clear as day. What was more, she had plenty of other reasons to hate me too. She might well put poison in my food tomorrow. 'Listen, have it out with her first, come downstairs and talk to her, I'm sure it can all be explained – it must all have been Fräulein Fricke's fault.' At that moment Franz revolted me – revolted me so much I couldn't even have brought myself to slap his face. His mother had tormented him for years, he'd never had a moment's happiness with her, and now here he was suddenly standing up for her, protecting her. Why? Because she'd treated him badly? Because she was his mother? I ask you! Well, a man like that had just better live with his mother and do without all other women.

I still feel like throwing up when I think how Aunt Adelheid carried on because I'd stolen her only son. But she was all in favour of the war. She would have had no objection to her son's falling in war. It was just that she didn't want any other woman to have him. And Aunt Adelheid's not the only mother of this sort; Gerti could tell a tale or so along the same lines. An old man never gets as nasty and venomous as an old woman.

Franz carried my case to the station. I wasn't speaking to him. We sat over a glass of beer in the waiting room for fifty minutes. I still wasn't speaking to him.

He handed my case up to me in the train, and I didn't speak to him. When the train started, I looked out of the window without waving.

I saw Franz standing on the platform looking sad and lonely.

A few minutes later I could have wept because I hadn't waved. Honestly, I was out of my mind!

The further the train got from Cologne, the happier and more relieved I felt. I had the impression that at last I'd been saved from every danger that could threaten me.

I couldn't help thinking of nice Frau Grautisch, and how right what she said was. I'd send her a postcard from Frankfurt.

Frau Grautisch lived near us in Cologne. She was at daggers drawn with Aunt Adelheid, and friends with me. I'd run into her only a couple of days before, when she was fetching a litre of beer from the Päffgen Bar. 'For my Miebes,' she told me. 'Once he's put that lot inside him he'll be ready for his bed. I don't mind him drinking twice what he's used to these days, just as long as he doesn't go out to the pub. A woman who loves her husband and wants to keep him isn't letting him out to the pub, not these days. Liable to shoot their mouths off, men are, here in Cologne. And when they've had a few they *will* start on about those stupid politics, cracking jokes and making filthy remarks, thinking it's all among friends. Then they wake up next day with a thick head, and some jealous person or other whose business isn't doing well will have gone chasing off to the Gestapo or some Party office or what-have-you to inform on them. When I get home now, Sanna, I'll find my old man sitting there grumbling. "Elvira," he says, "this place is no better than a concentration camp." "Fancy you not noticing that before," says I. "We're all in a concentration camp, the whole nation is, it's only the Government can go running around free."'

And then I began an entirely new life in Frankfurt, with Algin and Liska. Like nothing I'd ever known before. It was a pity there was always something political going on here, too.

I wrote to Franz, and Franz wrote to me. He writes exactly the way he talks – not much. And I didn't really mind, because I was doing so many new things and meeting so many new people, who were all very nice to me – quite different from the crowd I'd had the bad luck to fall in with when I first came to Cologne. I wasn't interested in getting married in a hurry any more either. Plenty of time for that. I'm still young, and so is Franz. And it's four months since I heard from Franz at all. He suddenly stopped writing. I did notice, and I sometimes wondered why, but not often. There were always so many other things to occupy my mind. I wrote once, asking what the matter was, but I didn't care much when I got no answer.

And now, today, this letter came! My heart beat fast when I read it, and I felt a bit guilty, though Franz did stop writing first. I'd always had a vague sort of feeling that something was wrong. But now he's coming to Frankfurt. He couldn't come to Frankfurt if he were ill. Anyway, I can't think of anything but Liska's big party till after tomorrow. The party's tomorrow evening, and I'll have to work like mad, flat out, from tomorrow morning onwards. We're going to move all the furniture in the apartment round. And Liska's given me a dress for the party, made of pink silk, with a dark red velvet ribbon round the waist. Dear Liska. She's always so kind to me. And I promised her I'd go and talk to Heini.

FIVE

'Good evening Herr Heini – thank goodness you're here.'

'Evening, Sanna. Come and sit down, Dr Breslauer will be delighted. And how's our beautiful barbarian Liska, and that sourpuss Betty?'

The customers in here sit on narrow wooden benches at bare, brown, wooden tables. At least you can't carelessly burn a hole in the tablecloth with your cigarette when you're feeling tired. The place is full of buzzing voices and clouds of blue-grey smoke. Heini orders me a glass of beer and a Steinhäger – 'You can leave it if you don't like it' – and goes on talking to Breslauer, who is a Jew and a doctor of medicine and a friend of Heini's. Dr Breslauer has rather weary, clouded brown eyes, and a bald patch with a very few fair hairs left over it. Even those few hairs can still give him dandruff; you wouldn't think it possible. In five days' time he's going to Rotterdam and then on to America. But he's coming to the party tomorrow.

'How can you be true? . . . Oh, the truth is not in you . . .' Toni the fat queer is sitting by the bar playing his guitar and singing. He doesn't sing all that well, but it's exciting. At least, *I* like to hear him.

Heini is forty, and used to be a well-known journalist. He hardly writes at all these days – for political reasons, again. He hasn't any money, but he can always find people who'll give him something and feel pleased and honoured if he lets them sit with him. All his acquaintances are fond of him, though he can be very nasty and sharp-tongued.

He is forty years old, and not much taller than me, which makes him short for a man. He's not exactly fat, but sort of square. His hair is soft and brown; his grey eyes have a silvery gleam in them, the kind you only see in a heavy drinker's eyes.

I know about that from people at home on the Mosel. It can look very attractive in the evening, and I'd like a gleam such as that in my own eyes, but I can't take that amount of liquor. Everybody calls him Heini, or Herr Heini, because that was how he always used to sign his famous articles. Hardly anybody knows his surname.

He came to Frankfurt six months ago. He has all sorts of friends and acquaintances here, and they talk politics. He's collecting material about the German nation. He knew Algin before, too, and that's how Liska got to meet him. We met several times a week for months on end, and it never occurred to Liska to fall in love with Heini. She was interested in any number of other people, not a bit in him.

And now she's so deeply in love it makes her ill. She loves him madly. The entire party tomorrow is for Heini, so he can see her in a pink evening dress, with her arms and most of her bosom bare, wearing her best spangly jewellery. She thinks he'll suddenly see her in a completely new light, and his eyes will finally be opened, and he'll fall in love with her, something he has failed to do so far. She read somewhere that a woman in everyday clothes is a very different creature from a woman in evening dress, which I suppose may be true. Anyway, so far Liska hasn't had any chance of letting Heini see her in evening dress, though she's been wanting to for ages. But nothing on earth or out of it would persuade Heini to go to the opera or make a date to meet in an elegant bar. And you can't go to the 'Squirrel' or the 'Munich Taproom' in evening dress – at least, if you did, I should think it would look very funny. So that's why the party had to be arranged.

It's all the fault of a dream that Liska suddenly fell so madly in love. A dream and Betty Raff. Right from the start, I thought Betty Raff was even more dangerous than Aunt Adelheid, though you can never really say anything bad about her. She is tall and thin, with a very small head. She has a greenish-brown complexion, extraordinarily inquisitive brown pop-eyes in a shrewish face, brown hair combed back, smooth as an eel, and cold, clammy, thin little froggy hands. She is thirty years old, smells a bit sour and looks the same way. She works at handi-

crafts, making silver brooches and dishes. That's how she got
to know Liska, all of ten years ago.

She came to Frankfurt a year ago to pay a short visit to Liska,
and stayed with her, and didn't go away again.

Betty Raff bothers about all sorts of things that are none of
her business. She does it because she is so terribly high-minded.
She wants to help people and bring them together. She meddles
with everything, with the most high-minded of intentions, and
keeps people apart. Heini, who knows her, calls her the Poison-
ous Wedge.

Two people may be having a harmless little argument, and a
moment later they'd have made their quarrel up again if Betty
Raff hadn't come along to bring them together. People Betty
Raff wants to bring together remain lifelong enemies.

She's bored her way into Liska's marriage like a woodworm.
'You must make allowances for your husband, Liska, even if he
doesn't understand you. You're such a wonderful human being
– a marvellous, beautiful woman! He loves you, I really know
he does, so don't you worry.' And in fact Liska wasn't worrying,
not before Betty began talking about it.

Betty did exactly the same sort of thing with Algin. 'Will you
read me some of your work, Algin? It would make me so happy.
You know how fond I am of Liska – you have to try and
understand if she doesn't show any interest in your work at
times. She's such an enchanting child! All I want is for you two
to be happy together.' This was the first time it had ever struck
Algin that he wasn't happy.

He couldn't stand Betty Raff to start with, he'd have liked to
fling her out, but now he goes off to the study with her every
evening. She brings him things to eat and drink when he comes
home late at night, and sits in front of him like a worshipper
adoring a god, before he's even opened his mouth. She tells
Liska, 'I'd do anything for you! You must get some peace and
quiet, Liska dear, you mustn't let a man like that get on your
nerves.' And Liska is grateful to Betty Raff. So is Algin.

Betty Raff herself says she takes no carnal interest in any
man. She has it a bit wrong there, the fact being that no man
takes any carnal interest in her. Anyway, she went vegetarian

in early youth, with a view to improving her mind and rising to higher things.

Years ago, there was a small ad in a vegetarian magazine, put in by a lonely and deeply sensitive Swiss soul who wanted to correspond with a compatible, nature-loving kindred spirit. Betty Raff got into correspondence with this soul.

After the kindred spirits had been writing to each other for a year, and it turned out that they were entirely compatible, the young Swiss vegetarian came to stay with Betty Raff and her parents. Betty's parents were extremely fond of eating bloody beefsteaks, with which they drank beer. When the wonderfully sensitive Swiss soul came to stay, they were not allowed to eat anything but carrot cutlets and cornflakes, for Betty's sake. They stuck it out, too, for five days on end, though it was quite an ordeal, because they were hoping to bring Betty and this man together and be rid of her at last.

The hopes of Betty and her parents would probably have been fulfilled, but for Betty's younger, red-cheeked, meat-eating sister. This girl stole the deeply sensitive and also well-to-do young Swiss, partly by force and partly by guile. On the sixth day of his visit, Betty saw him sitting in a restaurant with her red-cheeked sister, eating knuckle of veal and drinking Munich beer. As Betty herself has said: at that moment something broke within her.

About four months ago I went into Liska's room one morning. Liska was still in bed, and Betty Raff was perched on the divan. 'Oh, Sanna, sit down and let me tell you too, it's very funny,' said Liska. Betty Raff frowned. She doesn't like anything to be funny, and she doesn't like anyone but herself to be told a thing in confidence. I thought, straight off, that Liska was going to tell us another of her dreams. She has no end of exciting dreams, all colourful and confused, the way dreams are, and she always wants to tell someone about them at once. Well, Algin has plenty of time in the mornings, but he ceased taking an interest in Liska's dreams long ago; he doesn't want to listen to them. Myself, I think other people's dreams are a bit boring too. We all have dreams of our own, after all.

But Betty Raff listens to Liska's dreams with passionate

interest, and interprets them. First of all, however, she always says, 'Strange!' in a hollow and portentous way.

Well, that morning Liska told us she'd dreamed of Heini. She thought that was funny, because she'd never taken any notice of him or thought about him much. In her dream, however, she had kissed Heini, of all people, and he had been perfectly delightful, and possibly the pair of them went on to do something else, or so Liska indicated. 'Strange,' said Betty Raff. 'Very strange. I always suspected something of the kind.'

Well, I don't know. A dream like that, in itself, is nothing to write home about. You laugh and then forget it again. Good heavens, to think of all the things I've dreamed in *my* life! Not so long ago I was swimming about with Hanna Porz in rough water and a state of panic. Hanna Porz went to school with me. I was never particularly friendly with her and I never quarrelled with her either. I haven't seen her or thought of her for years. Why would I? Then I suddenly dream of her. And then again, I've dreamed of having a terrible fight with Liska or Algin, who have always been so kind to me. But in my dream, they were so nasty that I had to cry and I woke up in floods of tears. When I saw them at breakfast I was still feeling furious and didn't want to speak to them because they'd been so horrible to me in my dream. But it had all passed off an hour later. Perhaps Liska's dream would have passed off, too, if Betty Raff hadn't thought it all so strange and discussed it with her for hours.

We met Heini that evening, and Liska took a good look at him for the first time. After all, she already had a kind of clandestine relationship with him. What struck her most was that Heini was polite and friendly to her, but showed no signs whatsoever of being in love. So then she began paying attention to Heini without his noticing. That evening, before we went to bed, she told Betty and me she didn't understand her dream, God knew Heini was not the sort of man you'd fall in love with, in fact she found him actually repulsive, physically. Next morning she said she could be interested in Heini, but that had nothing to do with love. A few days later she was saying it would be fun to flirt with Heini, she'd like to see him ruffled for once.

But there it was, Heini wouldn't be ruffled. I think Liska's feelings for him *would* have passed off quite soon and quite harmlessly, if Betty Raff hadn't gone meddling as hard as she could again. She said flirtation was a worthless and degrading pastime, but she could understand deep feelings, she could understand a great passion. Liska, she said, was an extraordinarily passionate and deeply feeling sort of person – perhaps she herself didn't realize what she was suffering. She told Liska she had noticed something strangely mysterious in the air between her and Heini. I was on the look-out myself, but *I* didn't spot anything mysterious. Then Betty told Algin he mustn't take it too seriously if his wife seemed a little fatigued just now and not quite her usual self, he must be tender and considerate and it would all blow over. Whereupon Algin asked Liska what the matter was. It alarmed Liska no end to think that even Algin had noticed something.

And now we have reached the point where Liska thinks of nothing but Heini, talks of no one but Heini, and is practically out of her mind with love.

She talks to Betty Raff about Heini from morning to night. And she is much afraid of Betty Raff, too. Betty mustn't know Liska sometimes talks to me and tells *me* things as well. Betty is more or less running the household now, and is going to get me out of the place one of these days.

'Toni,' Heini tells the guitarist, 'play us the song about the Count and his maid. Good song, that. You'll have another Steinhäger, won't you, Breslauer? More Steinhägers, waiter, and suitably Germanic pale ale. You do know I haven't any money with me, don't you, Breslauer? I ought really to order champagne, pay you out for wearing that dismal look on your face, trouble is I don't like the stuff. Do *you* like champagne, Sanna? No? Still, we could eat some goulash, eh? Do you good too, Breslauer. You've had a fair amount to drink today, you're not used to it, probably find yourself throwing up later. You'll enjoy the experience more with something in your stomach.'

> '*The Count lay in his fair maid's bed,*
> *He lay there fast asleep.*
> *And as the day began to dawn,*

The maid began to weep.'

'Come on, Breslauer, you join in too. Might cheer you up.'

> *'Give me a room, O mother mine,*
> *A room that's dark and narrow.*
> *Where I may weep and I may pray,*
> *All for to soothe my sorrow.'*

Breslauer tries to sing, but he can't. Heini's right eye is looking fierce while his left eye looks sympathetic. His brow is broad and grave and bared, his laughing mouth is mobile. I tell them about little Berta Silias, and how she died.

'Beautiful,' says Heini. 'Breaker-through-the-crowd number seven, fallen on the field of honour. Wonderful death for a modern German child, the parents will revel in it for years to come.'

Dr Breslauer is looking pale and upset. 'Heini, please! What a dreadful thing – a child of five! My God, the poor little creature.'

'Breslauer, you have been one of my closest friends for years, so I know your upright character, your mild but distressing tendency to parsimony – got to fight against that daily, you know, Breslauer, nay, hourly! – *and* I know your sickly-sentimental cast of thought. In three years' time that child of five, that poor little creature, would have been educated by the doctrines of the *Stürmer* to that high pitch of mental development where she could call names after you in the street and denounce you for attempted rape. Toni, let's have the song about the Count again.'

'The Count lay in his fair maid's bed . . .'

''S a matter of fact, I can't think what you've got against the race laws, Breslauer. Very humane indeed, those laws. Just imagine if Jews were legally compelled to sleep with National Socialist Women's Club members three times a week.'

'Give me a room, O mother mine . . .'

'Heini, my dear fellow, you know very well how serious all this is; can't you stop making crude jokes?'

'Not only, Breslauer, will I stop making what you call crude

jokes, I'll turn deadly serious. You're a doctor. I don't understand
the first thing about medicine, but a considerable number of
people, who would probably have got better of their own accord
if you hadn't gone meddling in your megalomaniac way, consider
that you cured them, you saved their lives. You've been practising in Frankfurt these last ten years, you've got a good reputation
as a doctor, and appear to have killed relatively few people –
no, shut up and drink up, and don't interrupt me!

'So you probably took the appendixes out of a few prosperous
citizens who didn't really, urgently need it. Doctors and plumbers
are tempted to go in for the same sort of harmless sharp practice,
seeing there's no way to check up on them. I have to believe what
I'm told if someone discovers serious and expensive damage in
my guts or my WC, right?

'There's one good thing, even high-carat gallstones don't have
the market value of diamonds. For I'm firmly convinced the Day
of Judgment is not going to be a pleasant one for the medical
profession as a whole. I dare say you'll get off relatively mildly,
Breslauer. You helped a good many people for nothing. I'll let
that pass, that may not be too bad. But your trouble is, you
suffer from attacks of sentimentality – it fairly provokes a man
to violence. How old are you now? Forty-three? I'd have thought
you were older. Ah, well, you never did have much youthful
beauty to lose. Breslauer, why are you trying to smooth down
the hair you don't have either?

'So you're not wanted in Germany any more. Can't practise
your profession, can't operate in your hospital. Your luck – oh,
very well, your deserts too, I'll grant you that – they got you a
job as a consultant in an American hospital. So you'll be able to
go on practising your profession. What's more, you will be
earning money and can live without a care in the world. What's
more again, most of your considerable assets are abroad already.
Think of the poor wretches leaving because they wanted to or
had to, with no money or jobs or influential relations. You feel
ill-treated, Breslauer, you feel you deserve sympathy, you look
on yourself as a German emigrant already. And fair enough too,
but you can't ask sympathy from me. I need my sympathy for
your thousands of poverty-stricken fellow emigrants. Jews or

Aryans, road menders or scholars, their poverty means they all have the same future ahead of them, and it has nothing, nothing whatsoever in common with yours, Breslauer. Later, you may stop to remember others who were driven out along with you, and you'll push the thought out of your mind in trepidation. For you'll be on the point of getting American citizenship. You'll be standing on American soil, strong and proud. What a country! Everyone is charming to you. Because for one thing, you've got money, and for another, you've got ability, and industry to boot, and for yet another you've got a gentle, friendly, yet firm disposition, which means you're not one of the sort who are disliked because they'll let themselves be pushed around; at the last moment you'll start to defend yourself. And moreover, you find actual sensual pleasure in going along with laws and customs and usage as laid down. You have a fortunate temperament, Breslauer. And money. What's the matter, Sanna, want another drink? Want me to get the slot machine to disgorge you one of those poisonous-looking chocolates without putting a coin in it? I can, you know.'

Heini has put his arm around me. His voice sounds so deep and husky, I could listen to him for hours. Sometimes I even understand what he means.

'And don't talk to me about your own country, Breslauer, because I can't stand that sort of thing. Your country is where they treat you well. If I'd been ill-treated at home as a child, I wouldn't have any fond memories of that home when I grew up. Anyway, you're a doctor because you like the job. Blood and pus, that's your own country.

'And if you're going to say another thing about the forests of Germany I shall rise from this table and walk away. You know you start looking more Jewish the moment the reflected glory of my Aryanism ceases to fall on you. You'll have plenty of opportunities in America to sit among anthills in summer and pick acorns in autumn – also, today is the first I knew of it that the romanticism of the Wandervogel lads was one of the joys of your life.'

I would like to go, but I feel too tired to get up and leave.

And here comes fat, friendly Herr Manderscheid. He is fifty

years old and runs the advertising department of a newspaper.
His legs are aching because he's been out collecting for the
Winter Relief fund all day. He looks exhausted and wretched,
and he's caught a cold too. Heini is delighted. 'Give me ten
marks, would you, Manderscheid? Doesn't matter if you haven't
got change, that twenty mark note will do. Thanks, Manderscheid, you can sit down. It's a shame you're not an old campaigner, Manderscheid, you're just an old member of the
People's Party – *were* an old member of the People's Party, of
course I mean *were*. Oh, you lingered too long, sound asleep in
the Venusberg of liberalism – and now, my modern Tannhäuser,
you're obliged to go round with your Winter Relief collecting tin
until it breaks into bud.'

Manderscheid gets terrified when Heini talks like this. He
would like to go, and then again he'd like to stay. He stays
because he's tired. He is afraid of Heini, he is afraid of the
government, which can take his job away. He wants to live. His
wife wants to live. His children want to live.

I am sleeping wide awake. My thoughts are dreams, my dreams
are thoughts. I was supposed to be talking to Heini about Liska,
but I can't do that in front of all these people. Heini's arm is
around my shoulders; he doesn't even realize it. How Liska
would envy me. He never speaks to her as informally as he was
speaking to me just now.

Cigarette ash is always falling on Heini's suit, and then he
looks all grey and dismally snowed under. When Liska is around
she sometimes brushes the ash off his clothes. And sometimes
she says, 'Do you mind if I pick that thread off your collar?' with
a kind of embarrassed laugh, blushing. But there isn't any thread
on Heini's collar; she just wanted to touch him.

Liska has never got any farther with Heini than the removal
of threads. And now she is as if she had broken into a hundred
thousand pieces, she is flying in the air like motes of dust. She
keeps putting herself together again in a different way, like some
intricate mosaic which she thinks might appeal to Heini. This
sort of thing is a great strain on a woman. And how is anyone
to know what Heini really does like, seeing nothing seems to

please him? Liska would do best to stay as she is. But what *is* a person, really? You never think you're good enough for the person you're in love with, anyway.

Maybe Heini happens to say, 'They're terrible, those showy big women with their ballooning breasts and magnificent Teutonic hips. I see a woman like that with a small husband and I can't help thinking of a cow with a flea hopping about on it.' The moment Liska hears that she shrinks, even her bosom gets smaller.

Heini may say, 'I can't stand that obtrusive poster-like style of health, like an advertisement screeching out the virtues of buttermilk and apple syrup.' He doesn't say it to Liska. He isn't thinking of Liska at all when he says such things. But Liska instantly turns pale, powders her face till she's even paler, thinks her back and her stomach hurt, and looks sick and tired.

Or Heini may say the only voices he likes are the clear, ingenuous kind, and Liska immediately starts talking in a funny, clear voice, opening her eyes with wide, child-like excitement, as if she were taking her First Communion.

A few days later, Heini says he feels worse hearing shrill, screeching female voices than having to eat stinking meat, a shrill female voice can poison his entire system. Shrill voices are corrupt, slovenly, uncultivated, says Heini. The voices of tenement dwellers. 'They're too lazy to fetch their kids in off the street at mealtimes, those women, so they yell down at them from the fourth floor. And what sort of voice is a poor female throat supposed to produce, then? I'll tell you: a woman's voice should never be raised louder than is necessary for the person sitting opposite to hear her.'

Liska has a lovely, deep, mellow voice. She had made it go high. Now, instead of dropping it to its normal deep pitch, she tries to make it as deep and hollow as an underground dungeon. And as hoarse as Herr Frockart's voice; he sometimes comes to the 'Squirrel', and he used to be in the police, but he got sacked for persistent drunkenness. No woman can switch to having a voice like that overnight.

Heini says women ought to be nurses: nurses are the only women who attract him. Liska immediately starts acting like a nurse, looking at everyone in a sad, gentle, pitying way, as if they were about to die of some dreadful disease.

And three days later you'll see Liska looking as if she were going soliciting along Kaiser Street. All because Heini happened to say a woman should have a touch of wantonness about her.

Over these last four months, Liska has been a completely different person at least thirty times. Not so Heini. Heini says women should work – Liska works. Heini says women are inferior beings incapable of sacrifice. Liska instantly looks as if she were about to stab herself to the heart with the fork she was using to eat goulash. Heini didn't happen to be looking that way, or she *would* have stabbed herself to the heart.

And now Liska has gone and become a mother and wants to get rid of the child. But it's not that easy to get rid of a child, even one you've made up. A couple of days ago Heini said a childless woman was like an empty nut – 'What's the point of her?' Unfortunately, when we were all going home, the desperately besotted Liska was walking beside Heini, and told him a secret: she'd had a baby eight years ago, an illegitimate one, before she married Algin. Heini was not in the least interested; he was hardly listening. He'd long forgotten what he said about empty nuts and so on; he said that a brave and responsible woman would take good care not to have any children in these terrible times.

So as a brave and responsible woman, Liska now wants to get rid of the child again. This is why I'm supposed to be talking to Heini and telling him Liska doesn't have a child after all, she only said she had, and the child really belongs to a girlfriend, and Liska covered up for the girlfriend's little mistake.

And I will tell Heini, too, when I get a chance, though it's quite pointless. The fact is that everyone *except* Heini takes a great interest in Liska's strenuous and exciting changes of mood. Heini has taken no notice. Oh, there *is* one other man besides Heini who doesn't notice her changes of mood, and that's Algin. Having got to know Liska the way a man gets to know a woman only if he lives with her for years, sleeping with her all that time – well, he's got *not* to know her again. It's like reading a wonderful poem, and learning it off by heart because you like it so much and you want to be able to recite the whole thing. And when you do know it off by heart you can slowly begin to forget it again. Which is what people generally do.

Algin is not at all jealous, because it doesn't occur to him that some other man might fall in love with Liska. He is not in love with her any more. However, their marriage wasn't dead, just a bit tired, something that happens to a number of marriages after some years, and something that can pass over too. And maybe everything would have been all right for Liska and Algin if Betty Raff hadn't taken it upon herself to save the marriage.

Algin used to like the fact that Liska's nature is that of the inmate of a harem. He hated women who worked if they didn't have to. Almost all women, says Algin, are harem inmates at heart, though they'd never admit it. Their minds work hard at living against their nature, which gives them touchy and difficult dispositions – and they take refuge in illness to have a chance of living normally and according to their real inclinations.

Liska would happily spend her life between her bed and a bathtub full of warm water. She doesn't like standing, she doesn't like sitting, she likes lying down best. So she sometimes pretends, to herself and other people, that she's sick, and then she can live the way she'd like to for a couple of days.

Liska wakes in the morning, and her bed is wide and soft. She doesn't want to get up, she wants to linger there, half-asleep, half-dreaming. The dreams she likes drift past her, bright and varied. It's only in the morning, between sleep and waking, that you have such power over your dreams.

Liska ought to get up to face a day which will give her no pleasure, because she is too idle for it. She does not like walking – not in the apartment, not in the street. All her stockings have holes in them. Frau Winter the cleaning lady forgot to mend them. Liska doesn't want to get angry with Frau Winter. She doesn't want to sit at breakfast with Algin, reading a paper which is all grey and makes her hands dirty and smells revolting, like paraffin. She wants to stay in bed. So she falls ill. Her voice is weak, everything hurts her.

We bring her coffee in bed, we have to keep all problems away from her, we fetch her cigarettes, and put her manicure

case and lavender water on the bedside table. We have to bring
her her hand mirror – Liska discovers some wrinkles on her
face, and falls asleep again, melancholy and exhausted.

When she wakes Betty Raff has to come and sit on the velvety
blue divan and talk to Liska about men and love, which comes
to the same thing. Now and then she has to bring Liska warm
water, because Liska is manicuring her hands. Slowly and feebly,
for hours on end.

At noon I have to bring Liska a little cold meat and some
grapes, and red wine, and then sit and talk about men and love.
After lunch Liska has a bath. It takes an hour. I have to fetch
her bath salts and powder, Betty has to find her towel and her
best silk nightie. Then we both have to sit in the bathroom – on
the lavatory, in the wash basin, anywhere – and discuss men
with Liska. Meanwhile Frau Winter is doing Liska's room.

Liska gets back into bed. Frau Winter has to draw the blue
curtains – soft, inky-blue light fills the room. It is a room that
looks round, without any corners to it. The bed seems to be
round, and so does all the furniture. Even the smell of the room
seems round and soft – all sounds, all voices are rounded. The
sound of a car's horn out in the street rolls into the room like a
soft, feathery ball.

Liska discusses men and love with Frau Winter. Frau Winter
is an expert on the subject. She goes into a great many house-
holds, and hears about the wives' problems with their husbands,
since they almost all confide in her. She is hard of hearing, but
she always manages to get the general drift of it. She is small
and quick-moving, with red hair and broad, pale lips. Her glances
and her footsteps are rapid. She used to work for grand folk,
countesses and so on, and she knows about men, and the beauty
of the feminine form and how to enhance it. She is devoted to
Liska, runs errands for her, would do anything for her.

We have to bring plenty of coffee to Liska's room in the
afternoon, and brandy and cakes. Frau Winter has to stay in the
room, Betty Raff and I have to be there, Gerti has to be
summoned by telephone. Liska's room is full of women, all of
whom have to discuss men and love with her. And in the round
and inky-blue twilight of the room, all the women gradually find

themselves saying things they certainly wouldn't say in the broad, bright light of day. I always used to feel embarrassed by these conversations, but now I'm more or less used to it, and they are interesting and instructive, anyway. Liska gets happier and happier. She's never so well as when she is ill. She's a queen on a throne of white pillows. She laughs, and loves everyone. Frau Winter has to get scarves and silk camisoles out of the wardrobe, and Liska gives them away to everyone who happens to be there. And she gives everyone exactly what they'd have liked to have.

If it were all to go according to Liska's wishes, her husband would come home in the evening and ask, 'Darling, what would you like, what can I do for you?' And he would ask the other women, 'Doesn't my Liska look lovely, doesn't she look enchanting even when she's ill?' He would kiss her and sit on her bed, and Liska would be glad to have everyone see a man thinking she looks lovely, adoring her. Her voice would go soft and tender, she'd put her hand on Algin's shoulder and admire it, so pretty and white on the dark fabric of his suit.

She wants all the women to go away at this point, and to have Algin become more loving than ever. She wants him to read aloud from his new novel and ask her opinion, which is to be more important to him than anyone else's. For Liska really is very clever, all the men say so, even Heini. It's just that she isn't keen on doing much thinking. So she wants Algin to stop reading aloud quite soon, and just be loving and adore Liska.

That's the kind of life Liska likes. Given a life of that kind she'd be happy and delightful and faithful to her husband.

But how can a woman live like that, these days? She has to read the papers and think about politics. She has to vote, and listen to speeches on the radio. She has to go to poison gas drill, and prepare for the war. She has to learn to do something so that she can work and earn money.

Liska learned to do handicrafts. She makes stuffed toy animals, wonderfully comical animals: fat cows made of dirndl skirt fabric, flowered elephants, tartan cats with squinting goggle-eyes. 'Drunk and disorderly phantom animals,' Heini calls them,

and he likes Liska to bring her new animals to show him. So
now Liska is really making all these animals for Heini's sake,
even if she thinks she does it to earn money and lead a useful
life.

Indeed, the life Liska's been living for some time must be a
great trial to her. Algin talks of nothing but politics. He has lost
any interest in admiring Liska and kissing her. The National
Socialists burned Algin's book. Algin has to write stories which
Liska thinks are stupid. All of a sudden he's ceased to be a
wonderful writer. As a matter of fact Algin himself often says
the stuff he's writing these days is stupid, dreadful, but it still
annoys him no end when Liska says so. And now he is coming
to think it's not so stupid after all, for he has taken to expressing
himself poetically on the subject of Nature and the love for his
homeland which arises from it, and he has Betty Raff to admire
him.

'The Count lay in his fair maid's bed . . .'

Heini is drinking. Everybody else is tired, but this is the time
of day when he is liveliest. Words roll out of his mouth, words
come pounding out of his mouth, he sends waves of words
rippling over the table. 'I'm telling you again, Breslauer, disease
is your element, disease is your native land. And you'll find
disease all over the world, there'll be disease around as long as
you live. Don't you tell me you think wandering around the
Taunus more interesting than wandering kidneys and cancerous
tumours. And don't you tell me doctors are motivated by a love
for humanity, either. Most good doctors don't care much about
helping people. Disease is what they care about. Good thing
too. That's the only way they really *can* help people. What use
would a surgeon be if his hands were shaking with sympathy?
A sensitive doctor's a bad doctor. Thank God, you usually
confine your sickening sentimentality to the pub, Breslauer.
Same as your colleague, that surgeon, what's his name?
Kunitzer, that's it. Where's he nowadays? England? Bully for
England. He's the right sort. Sober and cold as a modern
refrigerator in his professional attitude. Remember when you
took me to the hospital and Kunitzer was demonstrating the
removal of an appendix? Going to take it out in three or four

minutes, he was planning to set a world record for removing an appendix, have an appendectomy event in the Olympic Games.

'Remember the nurses fluttering about that operating theatre like white doves? And everything shiny, white and hard and bright. And that wretched little piece of humanity lying on the operating table. An elderly, unemployed bookkeeper. Body all thin, grey skin looked dead already. And a careworn look about his belly, and feet with their crooked toes sticking up in a worried sort of way. But his face was peaceful. Wouldn't have looked any different dead from the way he looked under anaesthetic, face grave and clear under a network of worry lines. That quiet, motionless net of wrinkles was like a veil of comfort. And it struck me as a cruel outrage to go saving a man at peace. Saving him for a wretched, unpeaceful life. He was as good as dead, my own hand would have trembled for fear of bringing him back to life.

'But out in the clean, red-tiled corridor we saw a woman sitting on a bench as we passed, grey little mouse of a woman with dark, scared eyes. She was muttering softly, praying at breakneck speed, as if she had to say all the hundred thousand unsaid prayers of her life in a single minute. Soft, rushing eddies of prayer coming out of her. "It'll be all right," said Kunitzer's assistant, hefty, blond, beer-drinking sort of fellow, full of the joys of life. He stopped the grey eddy of prayer with his podgy pink hand, just touched the mousy woman's poor little shoulder with that hand and the mouse looked as if God himself had appeared before her, and all she lacked was the strength to fall on her knees. A smile trembled on her prayed-out lips. God went on. And we were among the accompanying host of angels, remember, Breslauer? Along with a few more folk, authorities interested in the setting of surgical records.

'And the woman started praying again behind us, remember? Maybe she had more faith in prayers than in God. If I'd been a doctor my hand would have shaken for fear I couldn't answer her prayers.

'Kunitzer's hand didn't shake, though. The woman's prayers were answered. The peaceful man was saved for further tribulations. And Kunitzer went striding down the red-tiled corridor cloaked in annoyance. The operation had lasted three minutes too long, wasn't a world record after all.'

SIX

Algin has joined us. He is sitting there, pale and gloomy, his eyes dark caverns, his pale hands lying on the table. He has had another letter from the Reich Chamber of Literature. There's going to be another purge of writers, and Algin will probably get eliminated. He might yet save himself by writing a long poem about the Führer, something he has been most reluctant to do so far. But even that might be dangerous. Because National Socialist writers might take exception to his daring to write about the Führer without being an old campaigner for the cause. Similarly, he daren't write a Nazi novel, because it wouldn't be fitting. However, if he doesn't write a Nazi novel that makes him undesirable. People still like reading his books, people still want to print them, and that's not right either.

'Might as well do away with oneself,' says Algin.

'Got ten marks, have you, Algin?' says Heini. 'Thanks, Algin. Who knows how much longer you'll have anything? That's not a bad idea of yours, doing yourself in, you should put it into practice. You once had talent, you were successful. Your life's a poor, shabby thing now. You made ridiculous concessions. For love of your wife and your silly apartment and your furniture and so on, you hobnobbed with people you considered inferior, wrote things that go against your feelings and your conscience. A poor sort of literary man you are.

'So now you're thinking of writing a historical novel, are you? It'll be the work of a eunuch, Algin. A writer in the act of writing must fear neither his own words nor anything else in the world. A writer who is afraid is no true writer.

'Apart from all that, though, you're superfluous now. This dictatorship has made Germany a perfect country, and a perfect country doesn't need writers. There's no literature in Paradise.

Can't have writers without imperfection around them, can't have poets. The purest of lyric poets needs to yearn for perfection. Once you've got perfection, poetry stops. Once criticism's no longer possible, you have to keep quiet. What are you going to write about God in Paradise? What are you going to write about the angels' wings? Cut too short this season, worn too long? They're neither one nor the other. Perfection renders words unnecessary. You write and speak to communicate your thoughts, we write and speak to communicate with each other. Perfect unity among mankind means silence. Every word is war, whether it means strife or peace. As long as there are words in the world there'll be wars. And when there are no wars left the word will fall victim to eternal peace as well. Better do yourself in, Algin, because you're living in Paradise, and when there's nothing left to criticize the writer's lost his livelihood. So do yourself in, or learn the harp and play the music of the spheres.'

'I will, too,' says Algin, 'I *will* do myself in. But there are others I must do away with first. Got to do away with someone lower than myself. Got to find him, got to look for him.' Algin is drunk himself; what on I don't know. Betty Raff will comfort him when he gets home. Perhaps he'll do *her* in.

Fat, cosy Herr Manderscheid is looking anxious. 'Who's that?' he asks. A girl is fluttering past our table, slightly unsteady, colourful and light as a peacock's feather, waving to Heini, and Heini waves back. 'Want to meet the lady, Manderscheid? She's a good girl, she's established her proof of Aryanism, she's a member of the Reich Chamber of Brothels, lives in the same boarding house as me.'

'The Count lay in his fair maid's bed . . .'

'You knew I lived in a low-class area, did you, Manderscheid? In about the most dismal low-class area of Frankfurt. In a gloomy backwater of a street behind the station. Breslauer once came to see me, spent half an hour there, suffered from severe melancholia for two weeks afterwards. The stairs are dark, narrow and damp, make me think of sinister fairy-tales whenever I climb them, dreams of robbers and witches. The room's a real nightmare. Just the sight of the pale wallpaper with its muddled flower pattern is discouraging. There's an old bathtub of cracked, greyish-white enamel where there ought to be a table, and a big wooden board laid across it which is a raw, pale colour. My bed's a kind of raised tomb, narrow metal bedstead, foot and head like prison bars, musty, grey, cold sheets. And there's a picture of the Führer over the bed, our little National Socialist ray of sunshine, calculated to bring light into the darkest room, warm it in a nice homely way. All the rooms in the boarding house are the same. Maybe you'd like to indulge your senses there some time, Manderscheid?

'The landlady's a Baroness. Baroness von Freysen. Fine woman. Sight of her's enough to freeze the blood in the veins of the strongest man alive. I have to get very, very drunk before I dare go home and face her. I slept with her once by mistake, that's many years ago, she's never forgotten it, though. Means I can live at her place on credit. That woman has a grateful disposition. Apart from the picture of the Führer, there's a tolerably conservative-cum-revolutionary atmosphere about the place, you get left in peace. Mind you, I could still have credit at a grand place like the Frankfurter Hof hotel, on account of the old days, but if I went to live there it might make people envious, Manderscheid here or someone else would denounce me for running down the government. We are living in the time of the greatest German denunciation movement ever, you see. Everyone has to keep an eye on everyone else. Everyone's got power over everyone else. Everyone can get everyone else locked up. There aren't many can withstand the temptation to make use of that kind of power. The noblest instincts of the German nation have been aroused, and they're being tenderly cultivated.

'All right, don't get agitated, Manderscheid, I didn't mean to insult you. You'll make up tomorrow for what you've left undone today. You've got a family. A family man gets timid, can't afford to be a man of principle too, not these days. There are a good few see their families as just the moral excuse they want for apathy and crawling. You gave me twenty marks a little while back, Manderscheid, so I can buy you another glass of beer. Drink up!'

The café's getting emptier now, but it is no quieter. The fat,

cheerful proprietor with his beer belly is standing beside us.
'Evening, ladies and gentlemen, see you soon, good night, *Heil
Hitler*,' he says to his customers as they go out, adding, to
Heini, 'Well, never know who you may be speaking to, do you,
or what they happen to like?'

'The *Stürmer*, new edition just out, the *Stinging Nettle* and
the *Illustrated Observer* for sale.'

Oh lord, I was hoping we could go home at last, and here
comes the man who sells the *Stürmer*, the character Heini likes
to engage in conversation, asking him ideological questions about
World Outlook. The *Stürmer* man is about forty, fair and pale
and tired, and bursting with zeal. He beavers away investigating
all sort of Jewish secrets; he's always discovering something
new.

Breslauer doesn't like it when Heini calls the *Stürmer* man
over, he is sliding back and forth on his seat in his uneasiness,
and his eyes flicker. 'Calm down, Breslauer,' says Heini, 'don't
you worry, the man has wonderfully well-developed instincts,
his blood speaks loud and clear. Anyone can see you're Jewish
– anyone except our friend from the *Stürmer*.'

Blue clouds of smoke fill the air, almost enough to smother
you. The proprietor is switching off lights at the back of the
café, the waiters are beginning to empty ashtrays and bang them
down again on the tables in a busy, unwelcoming way. Toni
tenderly wraps his guitar in black oilcloth and finishes the end
of his drink.

The *Stürmer* man has found out something new about Jews
and Freemasons, to the effect that our five and ten pfennig
coins have a sinister connection with Judaism and thus with
Freemasonry. The fact is that the stalks of the ears of corn on
the backs of those coins form a kind of Star of David. I can never
understand the *Stürmer* man's explanations. He says he can
now divulge that he is on the track of a shocking conspiracy.
'Amazing,' says Heini, 'I'd never have thought of a thing like
that. What an intelligent person you are, what a very intelligent
person!'

The *Stürmer* man is delighted. He looks at Heini and our
whole party with as much love and gratitude as if he were ready

to risk his life rescuing every one of us from a burning house. 'Oh, I'm only a very simple, uneducated man, ladies and gentlemen, but I've educated myself out of the *Stürmer*, you see. But for the *Stürmer* I'd never have known about the terrible dangers threatening our magnificent Aryan destiny. I'd have been blind to the whole Jewish question. I will say this, though, it's in my nature to have a deeply inquiring mind. I get it from my stars. I hope you won't think me immodest when I tell you I was born under Leo.' And the *Stürmer* man falls silent.

'Good heavens!' says Heini. 'Why, then you share a birth month with this gentleman.' And he indicates Breslauer.

'I knew it,' says the *Stürmer* man. 'I felt it at once – I sensed it! Give me your hand, sir.' Breslauer shakes hands, looking embarrassed. The *Stürmer* man is all emotional. 'I can tell, just from the look of you, that *you* have a deeply inquiring mind too,' he says. 'You will understand me. When two Leos meet, anywhere in the world, they're like brothers. I'll tell you something, as another Leo – something I haven't told a living soul before. Do you mind if I sit down for a minute, ladies and gentlemen?'

The *Stürmer* man sits down beside Breslauer and offers to buy him a beer – 'No, really, I insist!'

So Breslauer and the *Stürmer* man raise their glasses and drink to those born under the sign of the Lion.

Manderscheid says good night and leaves without anyone's noticing.

The proprietor puts out more lights.

Algin is resting his pale, tired face in his hands, cradling it. His dark eyes are fixed with thinking, looking inward.

Lovingly, carefully, the *Stürmer* man takes a long, narrow packet wrapped in white tissue paper out of his heavy briefcase. Lovingly, carefully, he removes several small, red rubber bands. He solemnly undoes the tissue paper. I can't wait to see what's inside.

The *Stürmer* man is holding a bare little twig, which might be off a jasmine or lilac bush, holding it cautiously and tenderly as a mother would hold her sleeping baby. And he hands the twig to Breslauer with tender, solemn caution, as you might lay the

most precious thing in your life in your best friend's safe hands.
'Thank you,' breathes Breslauer, holding the twig reverently,
not sure what to do with it.

'The fact is,' says the *Stürmer* man, after quite a long silence,
'the fact is, I invented it! Only you, another Leo, can really
understand. There are such people as diviners. You know about
diviners? They go around with a forked stick looking for water
underground. Hidden springs. Diviners are the elect, appointed
by the stars. The rod in their hands strikes the ground if there
is a spring hidden deep below. And then we dig for that pure,
Aryan spring, and the well may bring in a good deal of money.
Well, now – I have invented *this* diviner's rod for recognizing
Jews. You see, one can't always tell who Jews are, straight off.
The *Stürmer* writes that they're children of the Devil. Now the
Devil may take on all sorts of shapes. But I can find him out
with my rod! There are some Jews who don't look as if they are
Jews – and there are some Christians who don't look as if they
are Christians. I can find them all out with my rod. I take it in
my hand and ride in a tram with it, or walk down the street. I
touch people's backs with my rod, and if it jerks, that person is a
Jew.' Sure enough, the twig is beginning to twitch in Breslauer's
hand. 'You're my friend,' the *Stürmer* man tells him. 'You're
another Leo, you alone can understand me. I haven't told another
soul about my invention yet, I've got to try it out a bit more
first. I unmasked a tram conductor with my twig last week. The
twig struck his back when he was punching a ticket for the
woman sitting next to me – I'd liked that woman on sight.'

'But what happens,' I can't help asking, 'what happens if
somebody born under Leo is a Jew?'

'You're still young,' says the *Stürmer* man, and he gazes
gravely at me for quite a while. 'You can't really understand
these things as yet. Signs of the Zodiac do not apply to Jews.'

And now I feel like crying, because I really do *not* understand,
and I don't think I will when I'm older, either. It was only when
I loved Franz I understood the world, and felt happy. When you
love, you're praying. Everything was quite clear. I wanted to
be good. I think you begin doing things the right way when you
want to be good. And I think I'm doing everything wrong now

because all I want is for people to be good to *me*. I want to be loved, everybody wants to be loved; for a thousand people who want to be loved there may perhaps be just one who wants to love. Our Father which art in heaven . . . my heart is all a lump of grief.

'Closing time,' calls the proprietor, barking it out. He is Bavarian, and likes a bit of a fight when he's been drinking, but there's no one here for him to fight with.

Algin raises his poor face from the cradle of his hands. His hands let go of his head. For a moment, his head sways wearily, helpless and desperate, as if two faithful friends who stood by him had left him in the lurch.

Breslauer rises to his feet. He doesn't want to let the *Stürmer* man pay; the *Stürmer* man doesn't want to let him pay.

The waiter gets the bill wrong, right, wrong again. He wants to go home. He looks pale, crumpled, wasted. Even a good tip won't cheer him up tonight. He is so tired that he wants sleep more than money.

We are outside the café, in the street, disconsolate as unredeemed pawnbroker's pledges. We none of us know what to do with ourselves, we none of us know what to do with the others. A sticky sort of weariness keeps us together; we can only tear ourselves apart by force. We are all rather drunk, and have become set in our longings.

Except for Heini, who is still angry and wakeful.

There is a cool, rotting smell in the air, as of graves broken open. It is spring. All that is dead begins to live again. What for? Just to die once more? Pale, blue brightness is descending.

'Off you go now,' Heini tells the man who sells the *Stürmer*. But he cannot tear himself away from Breslauer, he is shaking Breslauer's hand with the fervent enthusiasm of a child shaking ripe cherries off a tree.

'I wish you hadn't made fun of him,' says Breslauer, watching the *Stürmer* man stride away, heavily laden, and turn into a dark side street.

'I knew it, Breslauer,' says Heini, 'I knew there was no helping you. You think anything human is touching. The *Stürmer* man is touching, you're touching, I'm touching, the old madam at my boarding house where I'm going back now is touching, Algin Moder the future Nazi poet is touching. A pity all these touching characters want to do away with each other.'

'And I *will* do away with myself,' cries Algin, marching off, taking long and desperate strides.

'Algin, wait for me!' But he doesn't hear me.

'Come on,' says Heini, 'come on, Breslauer. You're stupid, you know that? Just don't persuade yourself stupidity is a good thing.'

They've forgotten me. I was standing in a dark corner, listening to it all. They couldn't have known I was still there. All the same, they forgot me. They're all gone now, and I go home alone. It isn't far. It's my own fault.

SEVEN

'It's a lovely day, when you come my way, Marie-Luise . . .'

Dieter Aaron is winding up the gramophone. Gerti is standing beside him. Her dress is made of cornflower-blue velvet, her back is white and bare, there are blue streamers in her hair, she's a pretty, charming sight.

Coloured paper streamers hang from all the lights, wind their way over table-tops and chair-backs. Liska's party, Liska's carnival. Although Carnival time is over, Easter is coming and it's Lent now.

Everyone is on the move, their words and footsteps and laughter all lively and cheerful. Yet there's a scent in the air of a sad Ash Wednesday morning. Though morning is a long way off, it isn't even near midnight yet. It's only nine in the evening, and the nearby church clock is just beginning to chime.

'It's a lovely day, when you come my way . . .' Gerti herself is looking lovely. The dark Englishman's eyes are practically burning holes in her bare back, as she notices without actually looking. Every woman notices when she's being admired. Personally, I only mind about that if the man I'm in love with notices too. Men are so stupid, unfortunately, that you always have to point that sort of thing out to them. Gerti points it out to Dieter now. He puts his hand on her shoulder. Gerti is glad he will do something so dangerous. Because it *is* dangerous. I hope nobody has seen them except the Englishman.

'A lot of nice people here,' says the Englishman. 'All so happy, too.' He is drinking enormous quantities of Mosel, although Liska got extra whisky in for him specially this afternoon. The Englishmen arrived this morning, when I was in the very thick of preparations. Three of them, two young men and one old one. The two young men are slim and dark, the old man has a

clean, pink bald head, with little tufts of white hair around it.
They're all English journalists. They met Algin a few years ago
and have now come to see him and talk to him. They are on a
study tour of Germany, studying the change in the German
nation. They seem to like it a lot.

Algin wasn't in. He had probably gone to the library to do
research for his new historical novel. So Liska invited the
Englishmen to come this evening, and here they are. But Algin
isn't back yet. He's been gone since this morning. He *is* out all
day quite often, eats out and writes while he's out. But he knows
today is the day of the party.

I don't feel too happy when I think of Algin. I feel worried.
Why did Heini have to go saying that about doing away with
himself last night? It's not the sort of thing you ought to say.
It's not . . . Perhaps Algin has gone right out of his mind. Betty
Raff is worrying about Algin too. She is in the kitchen making a
herbal infusion to soothe her nerves. Her girlish evening dress
is made of bright green taffeta, with a hammered metal brooch
about the size and style of a breastplate at her bosom, the sort
of thing ladies of the olden time wear in Wagnerian opera.

'Have you got any idea where he might be?' Betty Raff asks
me. Her voice is shaking; her hands sprinkle a variety of
health-giving herbs into a teapot. The water on the stove begins
to bubble. Betty is vegetarian and high-minded because she
wants to be free of physical things, all pure and spiritual, but I
have never seen anyone so constantly concerned with the body
as vegetarian Betty Raff. I know drunks and gluttons with far
more time available for things of the spirit than Betty. 'I believe
an apple would do me good now,' she'll say, and she piously
grates an apple into a sort of mush and then eats it. Or she will
make an elaborate herb soup to heighten her vital consciousness.
If she eats three plums, she has to chew a quarter of a lemon
slowly afterwards. She goes on a special springtime diet in
spring, requiring five radishes every evening. Sometimes she
has to eat her vegetables raw and sometimes cooked. On
Sundays she eats wheatflakes and some kind of sawdust with
milk or fruit juice stirred into it. Well, you can't actually say she
eats, because eating is what ordinary people do. Betty Raff

partakes of her food. Sometimes she suspects that she is partaking of something contaminated by the smell of roasting meat, which would poison her bloodstream. Then she has to drink pure grapejuice and take spoonfuls of vegetable juices. She makes herself something different every hour of the day, and eats it in a grave, sad, reproachful sort of way, as if she were making a great and moving sacrifice on behalf of the crude, unheeding world around her.

Personally, I do not think Betty Raff is at all high-minded, though by now even Algin believes in her goodness and purity. Well, why not, when she admires him so much? She may be only pretending, but he believes her all right, because he feels abandoned by himself and the whole world. Where *is* Algin? 'We must look for him,' says Betty Raff, 'we must go and find him,' and she sinks into the shabby kitchen chair beside the stove. The whole kitchen is full of the wild disorder of a party. You only see a kitchen in such an untidy state when a party's on in an apartment, and this one is now a sea of glasses and dirty dishes. Teacloths lie around in pale and grubby little heaps. Thin rings of sausage skin lie on the kitchen table among cheese rinds and empty or half-empty tin cans. The rubbish bucket is almost bursting, overflowing with crumpled brown, blue and white paper. There are wine bottles in a corner, empty ones and full ones, a dark army of wine bottles. I wouldn't be surprised if they suddenly started to march. One poor, homely brown roll is lying in front of those dark, gleaming, erect bottles. I'll pick it up.

Good heavens, Betty Raff is crying. I've never seen her cry before. Now what do I do? When you've never seen a person cry before you can't imagine that they ever *could* cry. I feel awful, seeing this naked weeping; what *do* I do?

The ceiling light is flickering, weakly. Flickering down on the cup of greenish-brown herbal tea held in Betty Raff's trembling hand. She had better drink it. That great shield of a brooch at Betty's thin neck is wobbling with her desperately heaving breath. Up and down. There's a spot of grease spreading on the bright green taffeta dress, lying dark and round on Betty's lap, and she can't stand grease that comes from animal fat.

'Here, Betty, I'll get the spot out with warm water. Don't cry, dear, you'll spill your tea. Give me the cup – I'll put it on the stove.' This is the first time I've ever called Betty 'dear', but you've got to say something to a person who is crying.

I must spread a few more rolls, put champagne bottles on ice, wash some coffee cups, go and talk to Fräulein Baerwald and old Frau Aaron so that they won't notice Dieter and Gerti. Gerti has made a date to meet Kurt Pielmann in the Henninger Bar at ten; he mustn't know she's at a party with lots of Jews and people of mixed race. Of course, Gerti doesn't want to go and meet Kurt Pielmann, she wants to stay with Dieter, so I'm to ring Pielmann at the Henninger Bar just after ten and tell him Gerti's lying down in my room, not at all well, she can't possibly come out and meet him tonight because she'd be throwing up the whole time, yesterday evening really upset her stomach, with the alcohol and all.

Betty is still shedding tears. Damp cold creeps in through the cracks around the window. A spider is making its way down the whitewashed wall on long, spindly legs. 'Spider at night – all will come right.' Well, maybe all will yet come right. What *can* come right?

The tap is dripping in a maddening, irregular way. Drip. I count to seven – drip. I count to seven again, then eight, nine, ten, eleven – ah, at last: drip! I am freezing in my pink silk dress. It has a dark red velvet ribbon round the waist. Do I look pretty? Haven't had time to appreciate my own appearance yet. Drip.

'Stop crying, Betty dear, do stop crying. I'll go and look for Algin. I'll go directly. I know the cafés he visits when he's sad or angry and wants to get drunk. We could ring them up, of course, but he might tell them to say he wasn't there. I'll find him and bring him home. Now, you must go in there and talk to people while I'm gone, do you hear, Betty? You must sit down with Frau Aaron and take her mind off Dieter and Gerti.'

Betty raises her head. 'You must find him, Susanne,' she says in her thin, cool voice. 'You're his sister.'

'Lore, Lore, Lore, oh, see the pretty girls of seventeen or so . . .'

Where's my coat? I'm off to look for Algin. The apartment is full of gramophone music and streamers and laughter. What business is it of Betty's, crying for Algin? Liska ought to be crying for him. It's Liska's right to cry for him, it's Liska's duty to cry for him. If anybody's going to shed tears, it ought to be Liska.

Liska is not crying. She is sitting in the hall with Dr Breslauer, not listening to what he is saying, staring at the door with huge, burnt-out eyes. Because Heini hasn't arrived yet.

The hall is got up to look like a little taproom. We changed the whole apartment round this morning, so that it doesn't look like an apartment at all, but more like a kind of restaurant, though you can't feel as much at ease in it, as pleasantly unfamiliar as you do in a real restaurant, because it still smells like an ordinary apartment.

You get an apartment disguised as a restaurant and all the furniture goes into disguise too. The dresser looks big and bold, covered with bottles of liquor and bowls of salad and plates of open sandwiches and filled rolls.

A party like this costs a lot of money. Algin will have to pay for it. What with? He's earning so little now. Algin's got lethargic recently. Too lethargic to put up much resistance to anything.

There's a warm, insistent smell of roses in the apartment. Roses in bloom on all the tables, whole rosebushes growing out of big black vases on the floor in every corner of every room. Their dizzying fragrance makes my head ache. It's only just spring, it's the time for scentless flowers. There are snowdrops and bright little crocuses out in people's front gardens. And a magnolia tree outside my window, with fat, silvery-white buds among its dark and leafless branches.

Liska is looking beautiful. Breslauer's humming a song. 'Must I then, must I then, leave the town behind, while you, my dear, stay here . . .' He kisses Liska's hand, slowly, fervently. His foot lies on the floor beside the leg of his chair as if it had snapped off and was groaning.

The baby-faced old Englishman and one of the young ones come into the hall to have a beer after all that Mosel, and talk

to Liska. I have to call her aside for a moment to tell her I'm
going out to look for Algin.

Liska really is looking beautiful. Her velvet dress suits her;
it's the colour of a pale tea rose. Maybe Heini actually will fall
in love with her this evening. She is so alive, so trembling with
life, you can't help feeling it. As if her heart were beating in her
wide, dark blue eyes, her glossy black hair, her warm white
shoulders, her rounded little hands.

The dim light makes all the women's faces smooth and soft
and gentle, too. What was it Heini once said? 'Female flesh and
butchered meat need clever lighting. Good lights are absolutely
essential in a butcher's shop or a nightclub.'

'Liska, I'm going to look for Algin.'

The doorbell rings. Frau Winter opens the door. 'Sanna, oh,
my God, Sanna!' says Liska, kissing me with her full, hot, red
lips. There are crazy little notes of tears and laughter in her
voice. 'He's here, Sanna, he's come, I was nearly out of my
mind thinking he wouldn't come, Sanna.'

Sure enough, Heini's here. 'Good evening, Frau Liska,' he
says formally, kissing Liska's hand. 'Why, you look lovely, a
beautiful barbarian; are your ears bleeding? What – wearing ruby
earrings, are you? Most attractive.'

Nothing else exists in the world for Liska now, nothing but
Heini.

'Behold, happy is the man whom God correcteth; therefore
despise not thou the chastening of the Almighty. For he maketh
sore, and bindeth up; he woundeth, and his hands make whole.
He shall deliver thee in six troubles; yea, in seven there shall
no evil touch thee.' This was what the little man with the bristly
white hair and the grey, owlish round eyes was saying.

'Yes, well, the words of the Bible are very fine,' said Algin.
'Very comforting to people still susceptible to comfort. I'm not.
I'm dying slowly, cold, lonely, desperate. There's no hate and
no love left in my heart. I don't want to kill anyone, I don't want
to kiss anyone, I'm as good as dead already.'

I found Algin almost before I'd begun looking for him.

I went out of the building. The streets were shiny black, like

eels. Wet and slithery. You could see the breath of the sky –
fluffy white mist. The night was still like a house, I thought, but
its walls were beginning to shake, they would soon fall in, and
then we'd be exposed, naked, helpless, in the broad light of day.

I walked through the Taunus gardens. The earth had a damp,
mouldy smell of cemeteries and strength. A car's horn hooted,
a deep, firm sound – it was in my mouth I heard it, rather than
in my ears. I had to swallow it down. Oh, help me, God, I'm
choking. Not a star out. Car headlights, just a faint bright glow.
And then dark again.

A dreadful calm came over my heart, numbing my fear,
obliterating my grief. I believed in Algin's death. I had no
strength or wish to find him. I went into Bogener's wine-shop,
where he goes on occasion. I wanted people to tell me Algin
wasn't there, Algin had killed himself. Then I could have fallen
down dead or unconscious at last. Because I was weary to my
inmost soul.

But Algin was there. He was alive. Drunk, but alive all right.
Sitting there with an old man with a bristly haircut. I knew the
man by sight. He sits in Bogener's wineshop every afternoon
and every evening, by himself, circumspectly drinking half a
bottle of claret. I knew his way of beckoning to the waiter. I
knew his way of giving a tip. I knew his usual seat. I knew the
newspaper he read, I knew the wine he drank. I knew when he
came in and I knew when he left. I'd never spoken to him, never
thought much about him, but he was familiar to me, familiar and
unimportant as my big toenail. And to see him sitting in a
different part of the café talking to Algin struck me as strange,
mysterious and not quite right, as if my big toenail had suddenly
taken the place of my eyelashes.

'Algin, please come home.' Algin doesn't stir. He is talking
what sounds like a lot of nonsense to the bristly-haired man. It
takes me a while to make head or tail of it at all.

The bristly-haired man is called Jean Küppers. He used to
have a button factory in Krefeld; now he has a good monthly
pension. His wife was small and plump and cheerful. Her name
was Sabine, and he called her Bina. She had a warm heart, her
thoughts were simple and good. He loved her and always will.

So her death made him sad, but not desperate, because if you despair at the death of a loved one you are despairing of yourself, your despair rises from the suspicion, the knowledge, that you'll replace that person in your heart, forget the person and so lose them for ever. This was what Herr Jean Küppers was saying in his creaking, rather rusty voice. You could well believe he hadn't made any use of that voice for some time.

His wife Bina died ten years ago. That was when Herr Küppers retired from his factory and moved to Frankfurt to live with his son and his daughter-in-law. His son is a doctor. 'A good lad, doesn't drink and doesn't gamble, but don't ever let him treat you if you're sick, Jean,' Bina had told her husband ten years ago. Personally I think it's silly to say someone's good because he doesn't drink or gamble. If you stop to think of it, you realize what an awful lot of nonsense people talk.

Well, Herr Küppers gave his son and daughter-in-law a good deal of money every month so that he could live with them. But he never felt really at ease there, though he didn't consciously notice he wasn't feeling at ease. He didn't want to notice. His feelings were tired and apathetic. They persuaded him they were being very kind, doing him a good turn, him being so old and all. He accepted all they did and said, and he gave them money over and above the money for his keep every month. Because his daughter-in-law, Lucie, had all sorts of ways of asking for the money she needed and wanted: nicely, nastily, gently, roughly. She has pretty, brown curls, put in by the hairdresser, sweet, red, full lips, and a cold and tinny babble of a voice. Herr Küppers kept on giving her money. Not because he liked her but because he didn't like her, never had. So he had a guilty conscience, and that's why he gave the money. His son joined the SA – well, that was none of old Herr Küppers's business, was it? He didn't bother about politics any more, didn't bother about his family any more, didn't bother about himself any more either. He even thought his little granddaughter was vain and cold and unattractive.

Waiters in black and white were hurrying about the café; words and thoughts were spilling out of my head. Dear God, make me good.

Lucie, the daughter-in-law, wanted money for a new dress. He gave her the money; she bought the dress. It suited her. She looked a new woman in it. She entertained her husband's superior officer in the SA in the sitting room, just as thousands of young women before her had entertained their husbands' superior officers. She let him kiss her, just like thousands of young women before her, even though they shouldn't. It so happened that old Herr Küppers came into the room then with his son.

Old Herr Küppers saw all this as the way out of a dismal period. Young Herr Küppers didn't want to know. He was not keen on arguing with Nazi officials, and he thought his wife was a clever woman. Three weeks later, however, he decided on a divorce, because close scrutiny of her papers showed that she had a Jewish grandmother. He couldn't forgive that; he was ashamed of his wife. As for old Herr Küppers, he was now saying he found life with his son and daughter-in-law most distasteful. He wants to leave, he was saying. Today. He wants to be alone. If Algin likes, however, he'll take him along.

It is old Herr Küppers's seventieth birthday tomorrow, and that is what's brought all this to the front of his mind. He believes what they say about people changing entirely every seven years. Everything is ready for his birthday party at his son's house tomorrow, all the family asked from Krefeld and Frankfurt and Berlin. His granddaughter has learnt a poem, his daughter-in-law, with the Jewish grandmother, has been practising the Badenweiler March on the piano, his son has put off the divorce for the sake of the party, seeing nobody else knows about the embarrassing bit in his wife's papers yet.

So there is going to be a big, jolly, German family party tomorrow. Except that old Herr Küppers, aged seventy, won't be there. Seeing people change entirely every seven years, he's decided to make a quiet, unobtrusive getaway today. His pension will get away with him. That's the only thing his son and daughter-in-law love about him.

He got to know Algin this evening, because Algin was very drunk and wanted to confide in someone. He was going to do away with himself, and before that he was going to do away with someone else. This was the notion he'd taken into his head. I really don't wonder at it any more when I see people being crazy and unhappy. I only wonder at it if I see them acting like normal people.

Well, Algin wanted to kill someone worse than himself, or more stupid or generally inferior. He says he went looking for this person, but couldn't find him. If you've made up your mind to die you are very powerful, and Algin spent hours drunk on this sense of power, also drunk with wine on an empty stomach.

So Algin wandered around all through the daylight hours, but he couldn't find anyone to kill. He couldn't find anyone doing something bad, disgusting, ridiculous or hurtful which he would have been incapable of doing himself.

Then Algin wandered into Bogener's wineshop, where there were no other customers except old Herr Küppers. Algin got to know him by telling him he had the power to kill him – but not the desire or the strength or the right. And in this way the two of them made friends, which doesn't surprise me. These days, it means quite a lot if a desperate man, ready for anything, refrains from killing someone else.

'Got to throw my ballast overboard,' says Algin now. He has probably said this about a hundred times in the last hour. 'Got to throw my ballast overboard.' He doesn't want any apartment any more, doesn't want any furniture, any position, any riches, any recognition or any wife. Because the apartment and furniture eat away at his strength, position and recognition eat away at self-respect, and his wife's chilly lovelessness eats away at the warmth of his heart and at his talent.

So Algin is planning to go away with old Herr Küppers, walk off into the Taunus, along the Mosel, going he doesn't mind where. The world is beautiful anywhere. He hopes, even in Germany, he can earn enough as a writer and poet to sleep at an inn, eat bread and drink a glass of wine in the evening, without prostituting himself too much. 'For a poet who writes to human orders when his orders come from God is a prostitute.' I wish Algin wouldn't shout so. People in the bar are looking.

Algin goes home with me, except it isn't his home any more, he's given it up. Old Herr Küppers goes off too, to fetch his toothbrush and soap and a spare shirt. He will come to meet Algin at midnight, and the pair of them will go away and be happy and have their self-respect.

I am not supposed to tell Liska any of this. Why not, I wonder? It really may be a good thing if Algin goes off with the old man. Algin is looking old and wrinkled as a new-born baby, while the old man looks smooth and young.

Algin says Liska can have all the furniture, and the rent for the apartment is paid six months in advance. Yes, and what's Liska going to live on? What's Betty Raff going to live on? What am I going to live on?

'Lore, Lore, Lore, oh, aren't the girls pretty at seventeen or so . . .'

Singing and laughter spills out of the windows. A festive, gleaming strip of light falls from one open window, falling to the paved street below, dim and yearning.

I open the door. Algin melts into the party inside. I'm about to close the door again when a post or something comes away from the side of the building. Am I dreaming that the world is falling down?

Franz? Is it really you?

'I want to talk to you, Sanna,' says Franz.

'Yes, Franz. Wait for me, Franz, I'll be back in just a minute.'

I sit down for a moment in the hall which is now a little taproom.

'How happy the German people are these days,' says the old Englishman, the one who is all pink and glowing, and he adds, 'I'm afraid our train will soon be leaving, we'll have to go soon, what a shame.' He goes to look for the two younger Englishmen. They too are very pleased with themselves and the new-style German nation.

'How much better than when we had the Communists around,' says old Herr Aaron, pleased and smiling.

'I like to see the whole nefarious gang gathered together,' says Heini, politely removing his arm from Liska's clutching hand.

'What do you mean, nefarious gang?' says old Aaron.

'I mean this party is a gathering of jailbirds,' says Heini. 'Good honest citizens every one. Still, you know, according to the new German laws or National Socialist feeling or whatever, they ought all to be under lock and key. Pure chance if they're still running around here free. Or sitting around here free.'

'Wait a moment, Sanna, where are you going?' I'm going to Franz, that's where. He made me a sign to keep quiet, not to say he was here. What's the matter? There's a great lump of fear in my throat. No one is to know he's around. Why not? What's happened? He wouldn't come in with me, either.

Why is Heini holding me back? I want to get out of here. Liska has her arm around me, she is caressing me, her face against mine, her lips are full and tender, pressing into my hair – but her soft, emotional tenderness isn't meant for me, it's for Heini. My feet are cold and stiff with agitation and worry. My eyes see all these people moving about, my ears hear what they are saying, my heart is waiting for the moment when I can slip away without being noticed.

You can see the Englishmen dancing in the confused, disorderly twilight of the sitting room now, dancing in a business-like, tireless way like robots, among the blurred restlessness of the other guests. The paper streamers quiver in the hovering, curly clouds of cigarette smoke, the scent of roses fills all the rooms, hotter and thicker than before. If you close your eyes the scent seems red and fleshy, a physical presence – you could put out your hands and touch it.

Voices and laughter sound like the sea, a soft, rushing, excited sound. I scarcely have the strength left to raise my eyelids from my eyes.

I am dreaming this party, I am dreaming the dancing Englishmen, I am dreaming Mimi Baerwald's gurgle of laughter and the wail and the howl of songs on the gramophone – 'Raindrops, raindrops, on the window pane . . .'

I'm dreaming Betty Raff's shrill giggle, and the loud toasts being drunk by Algin, who is still alive. I'm dreaming Liska's soft, damp mouth at my temples. I'm dreaming the precise and doll-like mincing steps of old Judge Gleit.

I am dreaming of Franz standing out in the front garden, thin and cold, his face pale and grave, I am dreaming of his bright red silk scarf and his quiet hands, raised in warning.

I'm dreaming of my inward hum of longing for Franz, I am dreaming of my love. I am dreaming of my sleep, I'm dreaming of my dreams. I'm dreaming of all the wine I've drunk, and I'm dreaming of my helpless heart, embedded in a daze of weariness so that I can feel its trembling beat.

As if from far away, I hear Heini hammering out his words into sentences.

'That's right, Sanna, you can lay your head on Breslauer's shoulder. One racial offence more or less doesn't matter in this place tonight.

'Is there any more to drink, beautiful Frau Liska? Thanks very much. Your health, Aaron, you old lag. Glad to hear you like the new Germany.

'Young Dieter your only son, is he? Nice lad – a good fellow. Take another look at him – I'm not too sure about visiting hours in jail. Once he's in prison or a concentration camp you may not get to see him any more.

'What was that, Frau Liska? Oh, I'm not giving away any secrets, everybody here except for Herr Aaron knows young Dieter spent nearly an hour alone with pretty blonde Gerti just now. Frau Liska was kind and understanding enough to let the young couple have her bedroom for the purpose, and quite right too. Poor children, they were drinking champagne and kissing as they danced. Well, it's in the nature of things for young folk to kiss when they've had some champagne to drink and they're in love.

'Our little lovers closed their eyes as they kissed – well, almost all young lovers do kiss with closed eyes. They don't need any light from outside, there's a brighter, warmer light burning inside them. But these two enamoured children, Herr Aaron, they closed their eyes in the childishly desperate belief that if you shut your eyes and can't see anything, then you can't be seen. Children believe in fairy tales, you see, they believe they can cast spells to make themselves invisible.

'No, do stay where you are, Herr Aaron, it's better if I speak

of matters that concern you to your face. Don't get excited,
have a glass of this excellent schnapps.

'Well, what do you expect, eh? What can you hold against
your son? You yourself fell in love with a woman who wasn't a
Jew, years ago. You even married the lady.

'Anyway, your good wife has already seen to the separation
of our charming but criminal young couple; she did it with the
utmost moral vigour.

'What? Yes, while our sleepy Sanna here was out looking for
the lost poet, master of this household, her stepbrother Algin,
Fräulein Betty Raff was kind enough, in her own inimitable way,
to turn her attentions to your good wife, Herr Aaron. It pleased
your lady wife to describe her long years of marriage with
yourself as an unfortunate lapse. She expressed herself calmly
and with dignity.

'If I remember correctly, your good wife comes of an honour-
able but poverty-stricken Prussian military family, right? Forced
to earn her bread as best she might, working as a governess,
wasn't she? And you married her out of patriotism and idealism.

'You offered your wife the sort of comfortable life for which
she was certainly fitted. Your wife offered you an impressively
stern frigidity. And she gave you a son.

'You yourself were mentioning, in the most understanding
way, the fact that your lady wife is now sorry to have married
a Jew – or to employ your own terms, a non-Aryan. And the
only reason she doesn't get a divorce is because of your son.
She has now gone so far, in front of Fräulein Betty Raff, as to
deplore the impregnability of her own virtue, since in the con-
ditions currently obtaining, she would like to be able to hand her
beloved and treasured son the present of a little indiscretion
with an Aryan.

'Your wife doesn't just feel she is a proud, pure Aryan, not
any more – she now feels she is also a misused and humiliated
woman, and most of all she sees herself as the proud, heroic
mother of her son. She does love him. And she can't forgive
you, her wedded husband, for daring to hand on to that son the
taint of your race, which is despised and considered so inferior
nowadays. Your wife's logic, my dear Herr Aaron, is no more

confused than the logic of the Nazis. And the logic of the Nazis, I am sorry to say, is very little inferior to your own in point of confusion and ignorance.

'It remained only for the charmingly sympathetic Fräulein Betty Raff to point out to your wife the fact that her handsome, well-grown son Dieter was kissing his pretty blonde girlfriend Gerti. I am sure that Fräulein Betty Raff meant well by the young people, and she certainly meant well by the sorely tried mother.

'Your wife opened the unlocked door of Frau Liska's bedroom. Most commendably, Herr Aaron, your wife's lips remained sealed as to what her eyes then saw.

'However, that good Prussian Aryan lady expressed herself with indignation on the subject of the seduction of her good, handsome, Jewish son by a blonde Aryan girl. I dare say all this seems rather confused to you, my dear Herr Aaron, as well it might, and this account of mine will arouse ill feeling and dislike. I'm afraid I often rather enjoy arousing ill feeling and dislike.

'Very impressive and alarming, your wife was. I understand your son Dieter meekly let his mother take him away and send him home.

'Little Gerti wept. She's young enough for wild transports of despair. And she really is so deeply, truly in love that it'll be a good three days before any other man can comfort her. Breslauer has sleeping tablets with him, I gave her some, and now she's sleeping on her own, all rosy pink and tearstained, in Frau Liska's big bed.

'And your son Dieter is asleep at home, Herr Aaron. While your admirable wife is making cast-iron conversation with Fräulein Mimi Baerwald and an Englishman. Your wife speaks excellent English.

'Fräulein Betty Raff has now been able to turn her mind to her own concerns, since my friend Algin, master of this household, has deigned to honour this delightful and jolly party with his presence.

'Like me to tell you about the rest of the criminals here?

'Well, there's Frau Liska, inviting Jews to be her guests,

encouraging relationships which are racial misdemeanours. Moreover, she listens approvingly and with sympathy to corrupting and seditious speeches.

'Breslauer had his nose broken during the boycott in nineteen thirty-three, and was later robbed of his honestly acquired means of livelihood. He has ventured to commit the crime of sending part of his own hard-earned money abroad.

'And even your own optimism and belief in the boundless goodness of the Nazis, Herr Aaron, don't seem to have been enough to keep you from getting a little money deposited in Holland, just in case. You are also guilty of having once told a cheap but still seditious joke about a certain Gauleiter.

'And our good old friend Judge Gleit has not been able to refrain from criticizing justice in the Third Reich, or spreading rumours about the private lives of our esteemed triumvirate. Dear me, I'm afraid you've laid yourself wide open to prosecution, Herr Gleit.

'Another thing too – grown men, serious German citizens, have a very strange and comical look about them these days. When they get together they tell childish tales in whispers, pleasantly apprehensive, shaking with alarm – sad and merry tales about the great, that's what they tell. The conversation of our scientists, artists, businessmen and civil servants has sunk to the level of servants' gossip. They complain of their masters – and crawl to them.

'What's the matter now, Sanna – where are you going?'

No, I am not dreaming, it's all true. I must get back to Franz. Oh, for God's sake, here come the Englishmen to say goodbye. I'll have to let them out.

The three Englishmen are as cheery as ever – smiling, beaming, healthy. They're terribly sorry they really must be going now, but their train to Cologne leaves in half an hour, they're being met at Cologne station. The old Englishman, hatted and coated already, raises his full wineglass once more to make a short farewell speech. He drinks to all the ladies, and all the gentlemen, and above all to the wonderful, hospitable, happy German nation.

'Have you been waiting long, Franz?' Idiotic question, but you always ask it when you know perfectly well you *have* kept someone waiting a long time. My head is buzzing, I'm frightened, and I don't yet know what of.

Franz says nothing. I take him to the little shrubbery, it's only three minutes' walk away. There's a bench there where we can sit and talk.

Franz doesn't want to sit down, though. We are quite alone under the wet and dripping branches. Far away, the faint light of a lamp shines in the dark solitude.

I'd like to hug and kiss Franz, but Franz is acting very oddly, in a strange numb way, like something on a monument. I'm beginning to go numb myself. My mouth is numb, my arms are numb, my thoughts are numb. I feel no warmth or cold, even though I forgot to put a coat on, and gentle moisture is dripping from the branches of the trees and falling on my neck and arms.

'I killed him,' says Franz.

'Sit down, Franz – sit down beside me on the bench and let me hold your hand.'

So that was it. So that was it. Just a moment. I have to think, I have to listen.

When I left Cologne, Franz tells me, he was utterly if silently determined to have me back and marry me within six months. Slowly, steadily, he did all he could to enable us to marry soon. He'd saved up a little money. Not enough to open our small tobacconist's yet. And he realized I wouldn't want to come back to his mother's place. He wondered whether to move out himself, whether his small salary would support us both. It might have done, if we'd lived in a very modest way, but then we wouldn't have been able to save anything up and we'd never have got our tobacconist's shop.

And after I wrote to him about the prosperous, carefree life I was living with Liska and Algin he was afraid of making me live in such poverty, without any prospects at all. Because of course his mother would never have given him any money for the pair of us.

So Franz planned to stay with his mother another six months, have his board and lodging with her and not give her any of his

salary. He was going to save every bit of it, and put up with her
furious anger and her tears and shouting. She had plenty, after
all, and he'd given her all his earnings for years on end.

But things still looked very dark and doubtful. Then, all of a
sudden, they got bright and hopeful. This was all on account of
Paul – stout, round, funny Paul, Franz's one friend.

Franz is slow and painstaking and melancholy. Paul is quick
and enterprising and cheerful. He doesn't just like making plans
– he also has a brisk way of putting them into practice if at all
possible.

The idea of the tobacconist's interested Paul. He wanted to
help his friend Franz. And he enjoyed having Franz admire him,
and impressing Franz with his enthusiasm and skill. Also, Paul
wanted us to add a bookstall of books and journals containing
politically undesirable material to the tobacconist's, later on. He
was going to look after this part of the business. Paul had always
dreamed of something like that, and he very much wanted to
work together with the pair of us.

He had a brother-in-law who was very well-to-do, but quite
fabulously mean. Nothing in heaven or hell would have got so
much as three copper pfennigs out of this man. All the same,
Paul managed to squeeze enough money out of him for the
modest initial capital we'd need for the shop.

And now began a period of feverish activity for Franz and
Paul. Franz didn't want to write to me about it – it was to be a
surprise for me.

But once they had the money safe and sound it looked as if
the whole thing would fall through again. It was going to be
extremely difficult to get the necessary permits. Both men
plugged away at it until they were worn out. Even Paul ended
up looking quite pale.

Finally, after taking endless pains, they got over that difficulty
too. They managed to rent a dark little shop in a small side
street off the Old Market. 'Your Sanna will do it all up to look
nice and neat and cheerful,' said Paul. 'Women have a gift for
that sort of thing.' There was a living room and a kitchen next
to the shop, and we were going to live there. And there was
one more room beyond the kitchen, where Paul would sleep.

The shop had a gateway beside it where we could open the bookstall later. We'd have managed fine together. The room where Franz and I would live looked out on a little courtyard where white and slate-grey pigeons flew about or walked the uneven cobblestones, nodding and pecking. There was an antique dealer living near the shop, a widower who had gone in for pigeon-breeding after his wife's death instead of getting married again.

When Franz opened the window of what was going to be our room for the first time and put his hand out, a white pigeon flying past let a dollop of its droppings fall on it. Franz was glad, in his quiet way, since pigeon droppings are supposed to mean good luck and money.

Paul and Franz were more feverishly busy than ever. Franz bought me three geraniums in pots – a white geranium, a pink geranium and a red geranium. He and Paul negotiated with cigarette firms and enormous numbers of commercial travellers. And after much inward struggle and deliberation, Paul bought a wonderful nickel-plated cigar lighter to stand on the counter. The cigar lighter had a little blue flame that never stopped burning – like the haloes you imagine on the heads of the twelve apostles.

Franz and Paul had seen any number of tremendously grand and elegant tobacconist's shops – but everything in them seemed, to them, ordinary and uninteresting. While all *they* could afford was very small and poor by comparison, and yet to them it was a miracle.

Three days before the great opening, Franz and Paul were arrested. At six in the morning. Franz had been sleeping on the sofa at Paul's place, because his mother, Aunt Adelheid, was kicking up such a cantankerous fuss.

They weren't taken to any court, either of them, they were taken to the Gestapo room at police headquarters, where I'd been myself already. They were accused of undermining the National Socialist state. Then Paul went quite stupid with fury, and said it was his dearest wish to do just that, and he felt ashamed of himself for not having set about it yet.

The unpleasant little magistrate had Franz and Paul taken into protective custody. They were separated, so that they couldn't see or speak to each other.

The magistrate said leaflets containing attacks on the National Socialist government had been found at Paul's place. Franz doesn't know if that was true or not; he didn't get a chance to ask Paul.

Franz was asked if he was against the war, and he said he hated the thought of war. He shouldn't have said that. But it's totally impossible for anyone in Germany to know what he ought to be, what he ought to want or what he ought to say.

Franz didn't know why he was locked up, and when they let him go again three months later he didn't know why they'd let him go. He got no answer to any of his questions. They said things to him which he didn't understand. There was a flame of hatred burning in him that consumed all his thoughts. He couldn't feel his heart beating or his brain thinking any more, all he felt was that hot, burning flame of hatred.

'Where's my friend?' he asked. 'Where's Paul?' He asked thirty times, a hundred times. When his mind had stopped asking, his mouth still went on framing the question that the fear in his heart had taught him. 'Where's my friend?' And he realized he would never hear any more about Paul.

Franz put one foot in front of the other; his feet could still think. But inside his head it was all bleak and cold and untidily empty, like an apartment when the people have moved out. Franz's feet took him to the little tobacconist's shop in the Old Market.

There wasn't a shop any more. A shop with nothing to sell is not a shop. All the cigarettes were gone, and so was the proud and lovely cigar lighter with the little blue flame that never stopped burning. The blankets and pillows were gone too, and the rooms looked bare and stricken. The three geranium pots lay on the floor, smashed and broken. A red geranium, a pink geranium and a white geranium. But all three geraniums were dead, and were the same indeterminate brown.

The walls of the new little apartment were daubed in the most disgusting way. The sight struck terror into Franz. Why do people hate to see a nice, clean start? Perhaps it's natural to hate the people and the places you are robbing. You can't bear the thought that your victim is not a thief himself, and being just the victim he won't have a guilty conscience.

Franz falls silent here. His breath comes thin and whistling. His shoulders are hunched, as if he were trying to pull them around him like the collar of a coat. His hands are folded, limp and powerless. We walk up and down in the little shrubbery, up and down, up and down. Sometimes the headlights of a car in the nearby street break through the bleak blackness of the trees and bushes, like huge, hostile, searching eyes.

I would like to kiss Franz, but it's not always or in all circumstances as easy to comfort a man with kisses as a woman. 'Franz?'

I'm freezing. I wish Franz would notice I'm wearing a thin, pink silk dress, and I smell of roses, and my hair is curled. Well, the curls are beginning to come out of it in the damp air.

'Franz, it's all terribly sad. Dear Franz. But now we'll stay together, Franz, do you hear? We'll find a way together. Everything will be all right again.'

'It can't be all right again,' says Franz. 'You haven't heard everything yet, Sanna.' And Franz goes on with his story.

He stood by the window, on the broken geranium pots. Pigeons were nodding and pecking and fluttering about in the yard. They were fat and feathery and a soothing sight to see.

Then the old widower, the antique dealer who bred the birds, came out into the yard, rubbing his hands and letting the damp, cool morning air fall on his wrinkled old bald pate and into his mouth.

He saw Franz standing at the window, he looked all around him, cast quick, darting glances up and down the walls of the buildings, and then came slowly towards Franz and held out a hesitant and shaking hand. The two of them had never actually spoken to each other before.

'What was it like?' the old man asked in a hoarse, timid whisper. 'No, don't tell me,' he added, 'don't tell me anything, I know you're not allowed to – nobody who comes out of there is allowed to say anything. They took my nephew too, my nephew who helps me in the shop, and they kept him longer than you. He keeps quiet about it. He hangs out the swastika flag – well, you have to. We have to go along with it all, we want to live. They're stronger than we are, you can't do anything against them on your own.'

And then the old man told Franz that the whole thing was Willi Schleimann's doing. This man Schleimann was about forty years old and the father of a family, but he was always chasing strange women and girls who were nothing to do with him. He was tall and dark and well got up, and he wanted to make conquests of them all. He had an allotment in the Sülz district, of which he was very fond. He worked in it for the fresh vegetables, and because gardening is healthy and keeps you slim, and also because he could take girls to his allotment on summer evenings. He even used to shut himself up in his tool shed with women in winter. Besides this, he had a small tobacconist's in the same street as Franz and Paul's new shop, seven doors away. The business wasn't doing very well, because Schleimann had other things on his mind and his wife always had to serve in the shop. She was a glum, sickly, embittered woman, and put the customers off. Well, a customer is not going to stop and wonder what's made a woman nasty and unpleasant like that, why would he?

Schleimann was extremely nice to Franz and Paul at first. He went to the pub with them and gave them his expert advice on their shop. And he talked politics, saying things against the Nazis. He was in the SA, and found his uniform brought him more success than ever with women, and he was on the point of getting another pip when rumours began going around about him, to the effect that his grandmother had been Jewish. That meant he was flung out of the SA for the time being. The bit about the Jewish grandmother couldn't be proved for sure, so after going to a great deal of trouble Schleimann managed to get back into the SA. But his position was now a dubious and uncertain one.

He wanted to do something which would bring him back into favour and good standing with the Nazis again, and he also wanted to stop Franz and Paul opening their tobacconist's shop, so as not to have any competition in the street. So he went to the nearest Party office and informed on Franz and Paul for Communist intrigues and seditious language. It's easy enough to get rid of any competition this way. Unless your competitors stand remarkably high in Party favour, they'll at least get taken into custody for a while. And even if they're let out later because nothing can be proved against them, a little business just starting up will naturally be ruined and has no chance of recovery.

In the case of Paul and Franz, Paul had indeed said all sorts of things against the Nazis, and Franz had agreed with him. They were both so trusting. Perhaps Paul really did go in for Communist activities, perhaps they really did find leaflets at his place – how shall we ever know? But Franz at least knew nothing about it; he has no talent whatsoever for politics. His only talent is for love and friendship, and he loved Paul.

The old antique dealer was telling him what the whole street knew, for Schleimann himself had boasted, in the pub, that he had been too clever for those bloody Commies, he'd done for them all right. And yet Schleimann too had been an active member of a now banned political party not long before the Nazis came to power.

We are sitting on the cold, wet bench now. A chill runs up my spine. 'I killed him,' says Franz. I feel as if my brain has been numb and frozen, and is now gradually thawing out. I am beginning to understand, and to believe him. I want to hear more, more, more. I hear a tram going up the Bockenheim Road; is it the last tonight? I see the light go out inside a building, the grey, vaporous breath of all the sleeping people lies heavy on the city, it wafts over my hair, it settles with the light pressure of a veil on my shoulders. This is all so unreal. Am I still alive? Tunes are humming in my ears. I dream I'm hearing the music of Liska's party.

I put my hand in Franz's loosely clasped hands. They *are* his hands. It *is* all real, very real. Franz tightens his hands around my hand. He knows I'm here with him.

Franz listened to the old man. It was a cold, grey morning. When a ray of sun pierced the clouds like a sword, the old man hurried back to his own place, tottering along, without even

giving Franz his hand. The pigeons were nodding and pecking.
Was their hunger never satisfied?

Franz had been given his suit back. He had been given his
wallet back too. Franz counted the money in it. He counted
nineteen marks seventy-five pfennigs. He leaned against the
hideously daubed wall of his shop and ran his hand over the bare
counter. He had bought it second-hand, but still in very good
condition. Now, however, it had been hacked about with chop-
pers. Perhaps they'd been looking for money, or Communist
leaflets, or perhaps they just wanted to spoil the counter because
it wasn't spoilt yet.

Franz was filled with sadness. He was cold and hungry. He
tried to think, but he couldn't, so he gave up and let the sad
waves of his misery sweep over him. He stood quite still, waiting
for himself and whatever decisions his mind and heart would
take. Then the soft, misty melancholy melted away from him,
and he felt hatred in his body, hot and burning hatred, as if he
had swallowed the sun.

Franz went to the main railway station. First because he was
near it, and second because desperate people always feel drawn
to railway stations. And third because Franz wanted to write
me a letter which would get to me soon, though he didn't think
of that until he was in the station. And fourth because he was
already fleeing from the consequences of a deed he had yet to
do.

In the station post office he wrote me the express letter I got
in the afternoon. I do love him – he thought of me, and then he
entirely forgot me again. Women can never forget men quite so
entirely. On the other hand, a woman can never be quite so
steadfast as a man.

When Franz had written me his letter he went to a bar in
Komödien Street, near the cathedral. He sat there eating liver
sausage and drinking gin. He had seven gins.

'Just now Schleimann goes off to work on his allotment every
afternoon,' the old antique dealer had told Franz. 'He's digging
it over.' So Franz took a tram out to Sülz from Wallrafs Square.

He found the allotment. Factory chimneys rose into the air,
dark and tall. They were a long way off, but they filled the whole

view. The allotment gardens were a bleak wilderness of a valley among great mountains of rubbish. The waste ground was used for a tip, and the allotments had acquired walls made of ash, threadbare carpets, rusty pots and pans, boots without soles.

And in the shelter of these weird towers of refuse strawberry plants grew, with dark green leaves. Later they would get bright, white blossom and fat red berries.

Runner beans, with fresh green foliage and small but bright red flowers in summer, clambered over dilapidated little arbours drenched with lingering, grey autumn mists and the dull, stale cold of winter without frost and snow.

The door Franz opened was rusty. All the allotments seemed to be an ocean of rotting cabbage stalks. Here and there, white snowdrops came creeping quietly out from under the rubbish. You didn't see them creeping, just their whiteness.

Franz saw Schleimann. He was sitting on a rickety little seat in his arbour, right hand on the handle of a spade, left hand on the handle of a small hoe. The allotment felt like a graveyard where no one rested in peace, and it smelled of murder.

'You informed on me and my friend, Herr Schleimann,' said Franz, standing there in the arbour. A shiny brown box of face powder was lying on the floor like a giant beetle; a sweet and oily lilac scent filled the little place. 'Bloody women!' said Herr Schleimann, smiling to himself, and he spat.

'You informed on me and my friend, Herr Schleimann,' said Franz again.

'Don't you come bothering me, you stupid fool, get out of here, I've got other things on my mind,' snapped Schleimann, letting go of his hoe and reaching for an opened, half full bottle of schnapps that was standing on the floor beside him.

The schnapps flowed all over the floor. Franz's hands had a firm and merciless grip on Schleimann's neck. All the blazing heat of his hatred streamed into those hands, giving them immense strength. The spade dropped from Schleimann's right hand.

Franz went back to the station. He didn't take a tram, he went on foot. It was a long way.

Franz sat in the third-class waiting room, waiting for the train

to Frankfurt. He was not glad or sorry. He felt no fear and no
remorse. He had nothing to do now but wait for the train.

So that was it. He is sitting beside me, empty, burnt out. 'Oh,
Franz!' Telling his own story has not woken or warmed him. He
is frozen. He feels no pain, no joy, he feels no remorse or fear,
and he feels no love for me either.

'It's a good thing if you did kill that pig, Franz!'

He sits there in silence, head fallen forward on his chest – it
will fall right off any minute now, it will fall into his lap. As a
child I sometimes read stories about ghosts who carried their
heads under their arms when they went out haunting. The red
silk scarf flows over his bent neck like bright blood. Dear Mother
of God, they will cut his head off, they'll execute him. They
executed some Communists in the Klingelpütz prison in
Cologne. They screamed – I heard them. I was going to the
cathedral on the Number 18 tram – what's the street called?
What *is* it called? . . . Unter-Sachsenhausen. Thank God I
remember. Unter-Sachsenhausen. I was on the Number 18 tram
– why was I going to the cathedral? What did I want there?
When the tram was driving past the side street where that
dreadful prison stands, the Klingelpütz, we could hear the
screaming. Screams that made the air shake with pain. 'That's
the Communists being executed in the Klingelpütz,' said a young
SA man standing near the tram driver. He sounded proud that
he knew what was going on. I couldn't make out how we could
hear them all this way off. 'I knew one of 'em, quite a young
fellow he was, eighteen at the most,' said the tram driver. He
sounded proud too. He drove on, and the screaming went with
us. One man took his hat off in a gesture of solemn and devout
respect, as you might at the funeral of someone much loved and
well esteemed. He put it on again hastily, with a hand that
shook, when the SA man gave him a sharp, suspicious glance.
A child laughed, and its mother wept. One fat woman clutched
her left breast with both hands, breath coming short, a desperate
look in her eyes. The screaming still hung in the air, though we
couldn't hear it any more, but we could see it. We all saw it and
felt it, and for a second we were united in fear and grief. For

life had been taken, and we had been there. Then everything in the world was still. A young man got out of his seat, dropped to his knees and prayed. The SA man and the tram driver preferred to suppose he was mad, rather than have to rebuke him. They took great pains not to hear what he was praying. So we drove on to the cathedral, where we all got out.

Franz must get away. The thoughts are pulsing through my head, hard and well-defined, coming thick and fast and very clear. Franz has killed someone. When you have killed someone you're on the run, always on the run for the rest of your life. I'll run with you, Franz, I love you, where can we go? What was that whistle? A policeman? Is he after Franz?

All is quiet. That – what was his name? – that Schleimann may not be dead after all. Maybe he was just unconscious. But never mind how they find him, unconscious or dead, they'll be after Franz and cut his head off. He must get away . . .

'Lore, Lore, Lore, oh, aren't the girls pretty at seventeen or so . . .'

The gramophone is playing, I'm laughing, I'm singing, nobody must notice anything odd about me. Have I been missed? 'Oh, Sanna, here you are – look, here's Sanna! Oh, Susanne, isn't life marvellous?' Liska is drunk; she kisses me. However, she's acting a good deal drunker than she really is, so that she can behave how she likes. You have to be drunk before you can pretend to be drunk. She leans right over, to let Heini see down the neck of her dress. He isn't looking.

I must have a word with Dr Breslauer, a very quiet word. We have to get away to a foreign country, and I don't know how to set about it. What's the point of going to school if you don't learn these vital things there? I'd like to take Franz something to eat, but there's no time left for eating. Franz is waiting in the dark. I've locked him in the coal cellar; he mustn't run away from me. 'You've got to do as I say, Franz, because I shall kill myself if anything happens to you.'

We're in the living room – where are all the others? In the hall-cum-taproom? It's so dark in here; who put out the light? There are only three candles burning on the little table in the middle of the room. Heini probably happened to say he likes candles, and Liska thinks candlelight will make him passionate. 'We are dying, we are dying, we are dying every day,' chants Heini. 'Bit like a funeral here, eh, Frau Liska? Give me another drink, will you – thanks. Wonder why the schnapps is so warm?'

'Dr Breslauer, when are you leaving for Rotterdam?' I've got to find out how you escape. 'Whereabouts is Rotterdam, what country, how far is it to Rotterdam?'

Liska has gone to sit on the divan beside Heini; she puts her arm around his neck as if she'd strangle him in her despair. Where's Algin?

Just for a moment, Heini gazes into Liska's burning eyes, and he looks embarrassed and almost alarmed. Liska is crying, silently, without moving. Her face is fixed, tears flow from her open eyes. Heini strokes her hair, and Liska begins to sob quietly. 'There, there,' says Heini, 'what's the matter, then, Frau Liska? Can't turn life into a romantic opera, you know.'

We will go to Rotterdam. Breslauer is kind; Breslauer is rich. He will be in Rotterdam too in a few days' time. 'What hotel are you staying at, Dr Breslauer?' I mustn't say anything to him now, not yet, but I'll go to his hotel in Rotterdam and tell him the whole story. He will advise us, he'll help us.

When is there a train to Rotterdam? We must get away tonight. How late is it? Just on midnight . . . what? A train leaving at one in the morning? We must catch it. What else must I do, what else must I remember? We'll need passports. Where's mine? Nothing for it – I'll have to steal Algin's passport for Franz. How much money have I got? Oh, but you're not allowed to take money over the border, are you? Only ten marks. So what are we going to live on? Liska has some diamond rings she doesn't like, almost never wears. She'd give them to me if she knew what had happened, why I need them. I'll take the rings with me. We can sell them, later. And I'll write to Liska, explaining everything. I'll leave her my savings account book to pay for the rings. I must take one of Algin's suits for Franz, and a coat. I must pack a case. But they'll miss me after a while, they'll tell the police. I'll leave a note on Liska's bedside table, saying I have to go away, I'm in love, I'll explain later. She's sympathetic to anyone in love.

What else must I ask Dr Breslauer, what else . . . oh, Heini's talking to him. Heini's hand is resting on Liska's hair, as if he'd forgotten it. Liska is looking peaceful, almost happy. She dares not move for fear his hand will drop away.

'Yes, of course my life here's hell,' Heini is saying, grave and calm, 'but what would I do anywhere else? Without money or the chance of earning it? Without belief in God or Man, Communism or Socialism – without belief in change and improvement over the next few decades? I've loved mankind, I've spent over ten years writing my fingers to the bone, racking my brains, to warn people of the madness of the barbarism ahead. A mouse squeaking to hold back an avalanche. Well, the avalanche has come down, burying the lot of us. And the mouse has squeaked its last. I am old and ridiculous: no power or desire to begin all over again. Quite apart from the fact that I've never had an actual chance to begin all over again. I have said what I thought I had to say, in my own way, in my own words. There are plenty of others to say the rest of what I would have said for me. It's no bad thing, in these times of the general inflation of language, for a man to take counsel with himself and begin to hold his peace. I was a witty, humorous journalist. Can't be a witty and humorous journalist in this country or anywhere else with screams from German concentration camps for ever in your ears. There have been too many atrocities. One dreadful day, revenge will come, and it won't be divine revenge, it will be even more atrocious, more human, more inhuman. And that atrocious revenge which I both desire and fear will necessarily be followed by another atrocious revenge, because the thing that has begun in Germany looks like going on without any hope of an end. Germany is turning on her own axis, a great wheel dripping blood, Germany will go on turning and turning through the years to come – it hardly makes any difference which part of the wheel is uppermost at any given time. Over a hundred years ago, Platen complained of being sick unto death of his fatherland. Well, in those days you could still live in exile all right. It's different today. You're a poor emigrant. You'll find any other country is smooth and hard as a chestnut shell. You become a trial to yourself and a burden on others. For the roofs that you see are not built for you. The bread that you smell is not baked for you. And the speech that you hear is not spoken for you.'

What should I pack? We'll need everything, we won't be able to buy anything. What will we live on? I can leave that old blue dress here. I'll take the picture of the Virgin Mary. Shall we have a room where I can hang it? 'For the roofs that you see are not built for you . . .' I'm afraid, I'm afraid. The magnolia tree is coming into flower outside my window; it's so beautiful here in spring. My bed is soft and warm. I could lie in it and sleep tonight, tomorrow night, every night. My hands are shaking, my knees are weak with weariness. I feel sick, I'll have to throw up. I'm not well, I've got a temperature, I can't escape. Was that a ring at the bell? Perhaps they've already come to arrest Franz. Then I can stay here, it's not my fault, I did all I could, all I could . . . Oh, I am a pig, a pig! God forgive me for my sins. I love you, Franz. Everything will be all right if we love each other and keep together. Perhaps we'll die together. That's better than living alone and sad and spiteful like Betty Raff. But we're both young, why should we die?

'Who's that?' Case pushed under the bed, quick. How my heart is beating! I'm coming to open the door, I'm coming. 'Why, Gerti!' My God, what's happened? She looks dreadful. Hair tousled, her lovely dress crumpled like a dishcloth, her eyes red with weeping. She has been asleep in Liska's bed. Oh yes, I remember, Dieter Aaron has gone for ever, let his mother send him away. Frau Aaron is still here, I saw her only a few minutes ago. She was sitting in a corner of the living room pulling crackers with that fool of a student. She kept giving a shrill little giggle before a cracker exploded.

'Dear Gerti.' Oh, but I wish she'd go away. She sits down on my bed, weeping, talking. She would have gone anywhere with Dieter, she wouldn't have been afraid of anything in the world if only he'd been true to her. 'But he's only a weakling, Sanna, just a wretched weakling.' She hates him. She's going to write the Gestapo a letter saying she committed a racial offence with him, and then she will go to prison with him. Or else she'll marry Kurt Pielmann and be a Nazi and an anti-Semite. She'll pay Frau Aaron out, she will kick her and slap her, she'll plan an attempt on the lives of the Nazi leaders. Oh, dear God, I haven't got time to soothe and comfort her just now. Liska in tears, Gerti in tears, Betty Raff in tears – all in tears because they haven't got the man they want. I'm the only lucky one, I've got Franz, I am to be envied, I should be thankful, I . . . what was that? A cracker? No cracker goes off with quite such a loud bang.

There is screaming, the sound of running footsteps. 'Gerti – Gerti, what's happened?'

Heini is lying on the floor of the living room, with Liska sprawled over him, cradling his head. Why is she doing that? Everyone's looking at her. They are all there, Algin, Betty, the Aarons, everyone. I feel dizzy with shock and shame. Something shocking has happened, but it is something shameful too. All of a sudden everything is frightful: naked and indecent. I wish Liska would get up. A candle has fallen off the table and is burning away on the carpet, it ought to be put out, it ought – but I can't move. Is that someone crying? Breslauer is kneeling beside Heini on some limp roses, the tears are flowing from his eyes, while I feel like laughing aloud with hatred. I've gone crazy, that's what it is. I shall dance and laugh and sing my way to the lunatic asylum. Where *is* the Frankfurt lunatic asylum? You never seem to know these vital things. I shall dance out of the window, I shall dance down the streets, I shall – oh, do help me, God, do help me, Franz.

Streamers rustle beside Heini's head, blood is flowing over Liska's hand. Everyone and everything are frozen into a dreadful, bright picture. We are not living creatures, we are painted. Betty Raff's thin moaning is painted too. She is hanging round Algin's neck. Algin doesn't notice her. He is looking with heavy, thoughtful eyes at his wife, lying sprawled on another man's body. Crazy Liska. She has left a living man to embrace a dead one. Because Heini is dead, I know it. He didn't want Liska when he was alive – she oughtn't to be hugging him like that now he's dead and can't defend himself. Frau Winter the cleaning

lady has turned to stone too, with her quiet, hurried account of
what happened. 'Sick unto death of it,' he said, and added, 'My
apologies if I'm disturbing the party a little, ladies and gentlemen,
but I'm in the mood to do it now, I don't think I can wait a
moment longer. So goodbye then, and good night.' And then he
shot himself through the temple with a revolver and collapsed,
very slowly and quietly. Everyone thought it was a silly joke at
first.

Heini is dead. Franz is down in the coal cellar, starving. I
locked him in and I can't let him out again, can't move, I'm not
real, I am painted in a picture. Dear God, let a burning bomb
fall from heaven and destroy everything, release us all.

'Oh Rosemarie, I love you. I'm always dreaming of you . . .'
The gramophone is still playing out in the hall, I'll begin to sing
in a moment, I'll begin . . . am I singing already? No, it was the
doorbell. I heard it, everyone heard it. And the church clock is
striking – I'll count the chimes and then I will open the door.
Suppose it's the police looking for Franz? They'll never find him,
I'll lie to them, I'll kill them.

It struck twelve. 'Stay there, Algin, I'll open the door. Help
Liska, she can't get up on her own – for goodness' sake let go
of Algin, Betty. You go and help Frau Aaron, she looks as if
she's fainted. And give Fräulein Baerwald some of those drops
of yours to stimulate the heart, she's all breathless.'

The bell rings again. 'All right, just coming.' The door is not
locked, I only have to lift the latch. But I must be very clever
and very calm. I don't want to die. Franz must not die. I want
to go away with Franz, a long way away.

'Good evening, young lady, you're having a high old time in
here – that's about the hundred and fiftieth time I've rung. I
promised your brother to come and fetch him at twelve – is he
ready to leave, eh?' I've no idea what . . . who . . . oh yes, I
remember. Not the police, not the police. A cheerful old man
with bristly white hair and a Cologne accent. 'Behold, happy is
the man whom God correcteth . . .' That's him, it's Herr Jean
Küppers who was sitting in Bogener's wineshop with Algin a
few hours ago. It's his seventieth birthday and he wants to leave
his family. 'Happy birthday, Herr Küppers. Come in and sit

down. I'll go and . . .' What will I go and do? I must fetch my case, I must steal Liska's diamonds, I must steal Algin's suit and coat and passport. And there sits the little man with the bristly white hair, a small cardboard carton on his knees. 'All the luggage I need, young lady. Got to throw my ballast overboard, as your brother said. I liked that. We'll walk and drink and sleep and to hell with the whole world – I feel amazingly young.' I've got a hundred mark note, I've had it three years, I'm not leaving it here, it's *my* hundred mark note.

'Algin – Algin, Herr Küppers has just arrived. You fixed to meet him, remember, you were going off walking along the Mosel together . . .' I'll fold the hundred mark note up very small and put it . . . where? I'll hide it in my old tube of toothpaste. It will get dirty and ugly, and it's so nice and new. But I must do it, I must be clever, very clever – oh, I can't manage any more. When is it that train leaves? I will open the tube down the back, put the banknote inside and then close the tube again and roll it up and put it in my spongebag. It strikes me as very comic for a magnificent hundred mark note to be travelling in such reduced circumstances. But we will live, Franz! Suppose he's dead? He is dead now, he died in the coal cellar. I forgot him, I thought of nothing but our flight. I must pack bread in my case, I must pack meat in my case, anything I can find to eat. Franz will eat, Franz will live.

Everything's roaring and rushing, past me and around me. 'You can see he's shattered by his friend's death, Herr Küppers, he can't go with you now,' says Betty Raff. 'Lie down for a moment, Algin, take a valerian tablet, do – it will soothe your nerves.' And Betty Raff leads Algin into the study. He lets her lead him.

'She's nabbed him,' says Herr Küppers. 'Pity, that. Or maybe not. What sort of man is it can't keep an appointment, even one he's made with himself? Well, best of luck, young lady, you look the faithful sort, hope you are. Mind you, the faithful sort are unhappy often enough, but the faithless sort are accursed, they're *never* happy. Have you got a man, eh? Have you got a boyfriend? Have you got another human being in the world? Then you thank God and stick by him and be faithful to him.

Faithfulness can make women unhappy, but unfaithfulness makes them desperate. There's a dead man in the place, where is he? I'll just say a prayer for his soul, and then I'll be off on my way. A man renews himself every seven years, and I'm feeling good and young. Where's the corpse, then?'

Liska, I'm ashamed of myself for hating you when you were lying sprawled over Heini's body. Liska is sitting in my room. My case is outside the hall door, I hope nobody will steal it. Liska's face is beginning to wilt. 'I've got to get away, Liska, don't tell anyone – listen, I stole your diamond rings, I've left you my savings account book.'

'But why have you got to get away, Sanna?'

'I just have, Liska, I . . . oh, please don't ask me, I'll write to you tomorrow.'

'Here,' says Liska, and she gives me her ruby earrings. 'Sanna, do you think I can ever be happy in my life again? He's dead. I don't even know if it was *him* I loved so much. I just know I loved.'

'You'll love again, Liska.'

'You really think so?'

Yes, I really do. She has an untidy sort of soul, no man has ever been able to put it in order yet, I could wish I were a man.

'Good luck, Sanna, keep in touch. I'm no good at being on my own. I let Algin down, I left him to Betty Raff. I expect I'll have to go off and make toy animals now. Heini's dead. I'd have plucked one of my eyes out with my own hands just to hear a single word of love from him. Now he's dead, and I hate myself for being glad I didn't pluck out an eye. Goodbye, Sanna, God be with you wherever you go – and go fast, before the police hear of this. Breslauer will have to get out too.'

'Algin, do please take your jacket off, it's so hot in here you'll catch a cold.' Algin is in the study with Betty Raff. I must have his jacket, because his passport's in the inside pocket, and I need that passport. 'Poor you, you've been wonderful,' says Betty Raff, giving Algin tea to drink. He drinks in the words, he drinks up the tea. Liska will be leaving his apartment to keep herself by making toy animals. And Betty Raff will marry Algin. 'The prevailing chill,' as Heini once called her. Liska will be needing her rings for herself.

We travel through the night, and all the hovering lights go with us. My head is in Franz's lap. I must seem to be weaker than I am, so that he can feel strong, and love me.

I'm tired, Franz. His hand is resting on my face. That makes me happy. I locked him in the coal cellar, and when I fetched him out, he wasn't dead. Perhaps he had been angry, felt hatred, perhaps he had been full of dull, sad indifference. He didn't die, and that's love enough for me.

Is the border a line, or what? I don't really understand. A train stops travelling, and that's the border.

Men come along, opening cases, searching, rummaging – the border means fear.

The train goes on again, my hundred mark note goes on, so does Franz, so does everything except the fear. We have left the fear behind. That was the border.

So I lie in the dark blue racing bed of the night. It will be all right, Franz, I am happy, we're safe, we will live.

'The roofs that you see are not built for you. The bread that you smell is not baked for you. And the speech that you hear is not spoken for you.'

Franz's arms hold me tight, his breath is a torrent of love. The train is not running on rails, it's floating over a sea of happiness.

This seat is terribly hard and uncomfortable, but you are with me. We'll sleep now. We shall need strength when we wake up. There are still stars shining behind the misty clouds. Please God, let there be a little sunlight tomorrow.

WILLIAM McILVANNEY

THE BIG MAN

Dan Scouler is The Big Man, a working-class legend of physical prowess, fighting for his heritage – a decaying community in a small Ayrshire town – fighting to keep it afloat and intact.

'Inspiring and harshly funny. As in Orwell at his fiercest best, McIlvanney's outrage is all the more potent for being tranquil. Grand fiction that reads as truly as fact, (which says), "this is where we've been and this is where we really are"'
David Hughes, in the Mail on Sunday

'Confirms his reputation as the most incisive observer of working-class Scottish life'
Rob Brown, in the Guardian

'A novel of great power and microscopic observations . . . ambitious material, handled with sharpness and poignancy and full of memorable moments and images'
Isabel Quigley, in the Financial Times

'A prose of growing assurance, with vivid and memorable results'
Douglas Dunn, Whitbread Book of the Year winner, in the Glasgow Herald

sceptre

IRMGARD KEUN

The author was born in Berlin in 1910, and later moved to Cologne to train as an actress. She married in 1928, and published two bestsellers in her early twenties. However, as she refused to join the officially approved 'Reich Chamber of Literature' her novels were included in the infamous 'burning of the books'. After being arrested and interrogated by the Gestapo, she left her husband and escaped to Belgium. There she joined a circle of mainly Jewish and Socialist writers, including Stefan Zweig and Joseph Roth. She and Roth became lovers, and it was while they led a wandering life in exile that she finished AFTER MIDNIGHT, which was published in Amsterdam in 1937. Roth died a year later.

In 1940 Irmgard Keun obtained false papers and returned home to live with her parents. She had a daughter in 1952, but never remarried. Throughout this time, Irmgard Keun was still writing, but her post-war novels were not a success. At the end of the seventies, however, she was rediscovered and her reputation rose steadily. She died in 1982.

Irmgard Keun

AFTER MIDNIGHT

Translated by Anthea Bell

Copyright © Econ-Verlag GmbH, Düsseldorf, 1980
Translation © Victor Gollancz Ltd 1985
Translated from the original German, *Nacht Mitternacht*, first published in 1937

First published in Great Britain in 1985 by Victor Gollancz Ltd

Sceptre edition 1987

Sceptre is an imprint of Hodder and Stoughton Paperbacks, a division of Hodder and Stoughton Ltd

British Library C.I.P.

Keun, Irmgard
  After midnight.
  I. Title   II. Nacht Mitternacht. *English*
  833'.912[F]   PT2621.E92

  ISBN 0-340-40429-9

Printed and bound in Great Britain for Hodder and Stoughton Paperbacks, a division of Hodder and Stoughton Ltd., Mill Road, Dunton Green, Sevenoaks, Kent (Editorial Office: 47 Bedford Square, London, WC1 3DP) by Richard Clay (The Chaucer Press) Ltd., Bungay, Suffolk. Photoset by Rowland Phototypesetting Ltd., Bury St Edmunds, Suffolk.